DEVIANT-HUNTER: BLOOD OATH

AN EVE OF LIGHT STORY

HARAMBEE K. GREY-SUN

HYPERVERSE BOOKS, LLC

Cover design by The Cover Collection.

Print ISBN-13: 978-1-64044-004-3

Ebook ISBN-13: 978-1-64044-002-9

Published by HyperVerse Books, LLC

www.hyperversebooks.com

Crossing genres without apologies.

1

Half past noon, and the late spring sun had yet to crawl out from behind the heavy gray comforter above. The banana shrubs in the yard behind me gave off their fragrance just the same. Thank goodness my allergies were under control these days. I took a deep breath as I raised my gloved fist and knocked on the mahogany wood door. The doorbell had had no effect. The TV—deep inside, straightway from the foyer—was too loud. Some dumb sitcom. The retired chief of police was letting his brains rot with that shit. I hoped he still had enough upstairs to recognize what should be done with the gift I'd brought him.

The curtain behind the door's left decorative window moved aside briefly, long enough for me to see a gray eye and the heavy bags under it blemishing the pale skin. The door was pulled open slowly but all the way. The chubby woman had nothing on her but a faded orange tank top and jean shorts. No weapon. No phone.

"Mrs. Harwood?" I asked. "Ethel Harwood?"

She paused a moment to look me over, gazing slack-jawed at my goggles, the two-days-old stubble on my cheeks and chin, the scars constellating my face, and then straight on down to the jeans and boots before back up to the tactical vest. For this outing, I'd opted for the "stocked" version, the one without the gun and knife holsters; its many pouches obviously concealed more than a wallet and keys.

I was about a head taller than her—so it took a good moment for Ethel to drink me in. If she was a good wife, she was no doubt wondering if I was an ex-con from way back, here to take revenge on the former chief for some wrong. Part of that was right. But she apparently determined I was no threat to her—or maybe just decided she didn't much care if I was, considering I could do no worse than what had already been done.

"Yes." Her voice was as weary as her eyes. "You are . . . ?"

"My name is Sanders." I met her eyes and didn't blink. "That sound familiar to you at all?"

The woman shook her head tentatively as if this were a pop quiz and she was trying to guess how harsh the penalty might be for a wrong answer.

I continued, "You got a husband . . . by the name of Trent."

She responded with a slow nod, still trying to guess.

"Is he at home?"

Her nod gained a little speed.

"Ask him to come to the door." I again ran my eyes over the poor woman. She didn't even have keys on her person. "And make sure he has his cell with him."

Keeping me at least partially in view, she yelled over her shoulder, "*Trent!* Come *quick*! And bring yer phone!"

I heard footsteps almost immediately. Heavy thumping. The man had put on weight since I'd last seen him. At least twenty pounds by the sound of it. He rushed into the foyer, flustered. By the looks of it, thirty pounds. He thrust himself into the doorframe, edging his wife back a half step. His phone was in his front pocket. A Kel-Tec PMR-30 was in his right hand. He'd lost his physique but not his business sense.

"What's this all about?" He grunted the words, trying his damnedest not to sound as if he'd just ascended ten flights of steps. "Who the hell're you?"

"Name's Frank Sanders." I kept my eyes on his while giving him a slight but respectful nod. "You and I, we know each other from a ways back. You probably don't remember. There's no need to go into it in front of the missus."

"Sanders . . ." He gave me the head-to-toe lookover—twice. I guessed we were about equal in weight, though much of his two hundred pounds was fat. I sized him up in much less time than it took him to do the same to me; I chalked that up to age. "You didn't answer my first question, Sanders." An old, grizzled cop's voice tried to carry his words. It was barely more intimidating than him. "You're here because *what*?"

"Your daughter."

They both stiffened. I didn't flinch, not even when Harwood's grip seemed to tighten on the gun as he raised it by an inch or so. He started to say something. I didn't care to hear it.

"Ten years ago," I said, "your five-year-old daughter was kidnapped, violated repeatedly, then murdered. Body left in your front yard, at your previous house, down in Garth."

The wife went pale, seemed ready to faint. But something—something stronger than her husband, something deep inside her—kept her on her feet.

I continued. "Got a little girl of my own. I know how that

must have felt"—I fixed my gaze on the husband's—"especially when the police couldn't find the perp who did it."

The man tensed, looked like he wanted to start forward and start pistol-whipping. His type liked to draw blood before dealing a death blow. But he had eyes enough to see he wasn't a match for me.

"I'm not the Creator," I said. "Not even a re-Creator. I can't bring your daughter back. But I have brought you some gospel"—I hooked my left thumb over my shoulder, gesturing toward The Machine—"I found the bastard who did it. Brought him here to you."

They both gaped, looking briefly at me and longer at the tricked-out Hummer. The silver-and-black custom-built vehicle was larger and had more cargo space than the civilian version.

"I'm here today to present you with a choice, Harwood. Take that phone out of your pocket and buzz the local cops. Or walk over with me, look the still-breathin' son of a bitch dead in his eye, and dish out whatever form of justice pleases you all."

Ethel Harwood shook her head, her lower jaw raising and lowering like a schizo drawbridge. She probably wouldn't be the decision maker here. But her husband's face went through its own stuttering expressions.

I tried to be helpful. "I've got all sorts of tools in my vehicle. All very useful in a variety of ways. If you don't want to mess up your property, I know quite a few secluded spots in the vicinity."

Harwood rattled the contents of his cluttered head till he found his words. "Wh-who are you? I mean, *what*—"

"A ghost of the government." I smiled, tried to reassure them. I'm sure they were very familiar with the tired joke about the government showing up on their doorstep with an offer to help. Probably not that familiar with poetic idioms though. And honestly, I wasn't that good at them—so I unfolded. "Once a Fed, but I got fed up with non-results. Know what I mean? One result of my current activities is over there now in my vehicle. Shall I escort you over?" I backed up two steps and turned my shoulder about ninety degrees, accentuating the invite. Harwood looked at his wife; it was only a few seconds, but I could tell a whole conversation passed between them during that brief exchange. They stepped out onto the porch almost simultaneously.

I turned fully then and walked, not waiting to see who pulled the door closed behind them. Also didn't bother to see how closely they followed me. I could hear their breathing and—my training kicking in—even their heartbeats. The drumming seemed to increase with every third tentative step. I paused, turned to look at them only when I reached the back of the vehicle.

"Are you ready?" I asked.

They exchanged looks again, briefer this time. Ethel looked at me and nodded.

"Don't worry"—I unlocked the door—"He's trussed up like a wild boar. He can't do anything to anyone. Not anymore."

I didn't know if Harwood heard me. He had his gun at the ready. And frankly, I wouldn't have minded if he'd plugged the bastard as soon as he saw him. At this point, I was a quick-and-ready expert at cleaning all manners of body parts and waste out of my vehicle. But he hesitated. I kept my breathing even, unobtrusive, opening the door to let them get a good, focused look at Elroy, a skinny, goateed freak with jaundiced skin who—on his chest, stomach, and upper arms—had graphic tattoos of young children being brutalized. He sat on a tarp, clothed only in an adult diaper, his hands tied behind his back, legs extended and bound in front, neck manacled and chained to a hook on the roof. He was forced to face in the direction of the victim's parents, the secondary victims; but his wide, darting eyes couldn't hold their gaze. His whole body shook in the biting, arctic winds only he felt. Despite the fact he was tightly gagged, his mouth unceasingly mumbled what some might call poetry. He'd a gash on his forehead that had mostly scabbed over, a small token of my initial interrogation; his behavior, though, was nothing but a result of the drugs he was on. Street name was Jelly Raptures. Dangerous designer drugs designed specifically for kids. Yeah—this was the world I lived in. The world I *hunted* in.

Neither of the wizened pair said a word. After ten years of grieving, what could they possibly say? I took a deep breath, opened my mouth to encourage them—but then Ethel let forth, unleashing furious word-gusts that would've impressed a Texas tornado. A seemingly unending swirl of threats, profanity, invective, swears upon God and the saints' graves . . . Even my ears started to burn after the first two or so minutes. When she almost seemed ready to collapse, and Trent—to his credit—grabbed and held her tight, I met eyes with both of them. "Well? What's the play going to be today?"

Their lips parted, but they said nothing. Trent shook his head slowly before fixing a steady gaze on me. "Just how do you and I know each other?"

"Garth PD. About twenty years ago. I was on the force for about a minute. And then there was an excessive force incident. Or two. I disappeared. The rest, Chief, is classified."

He gave me a good look—up and down like before—

then shook his head again. "I don't remember you." Figured a bit of the man's mind was gone. Police work and losing a kid could do that.

"You had a lot of trouble-bodies on the force back then. I didn't stand out."

"Well, you do now . . ."

"I've come a long way since the old days."

"You . . ." He glanced at his wife. "You said, earlier, you said, we were to take out, *dish* out whatever type of justice would please me . . . *us*."

I nodded.

"Well, 'us' includes our little Jessica. The sweetest . . . gentlest . . ." His eyes went glossy. "The gentlest soul . . . I've ever kn—" He choked it back, tried to at least. "Well, Mr. Sanders, I . . . I . . ." He heaved a few times before sighing, feeling the burden of it all—history, progeny, profession, sworn duties, implied duties, honor, justice . . . I gave the man his respect, lowered my eyes to the pavement, didn't rush him. "I appreciate what you've done," he said eventually. "But it's not for us to do this man any harm."

I met his eyes again, then his wife's. The sobbing made her head shudder, but she clearly nodded in agreement. I nodded at both of them in turn.

"Wise decision, sir—for your peace of mind." I cast my eyes toward the well-manicured yard, then the house, a Georgian colonial. "You've really built yourself something here. You're doing well in quiet retirement. I reckon it's best not to jeopardize it." I looked at the miscreant, got a little less graceful. "As for Shakes, here . . . Well, if you've ever had trouble sleeping at night on account of what's been done, from this day forward you can rest easy that this once-human thing got what was coming to him." I closed the door, making it a little easier on them, underlining their spoken decision. "I'll make sure he's good and taken care of."

I strolled to the driver's side door, opened it, paused for a minute. I heard their heartbeats, their rate of breathing. I looked over my shoulder. Husband and wife were clutching each other's hands. Trent gazed at the gravel near the back left tire. Ethel at the tinted back window, her face tense, lips pursed, as if she'd been scrounging for any curses left unhurled and was on the verge of releasing them. They wanted this over, behind them. But out of sight did not necessarily mean out of mind.

I cleared my throat. "If you'd, uh, like pictures or any other sort of souvenirs for your grief, text me before next Friday evening. I left a card with my private, secure number in your mailbox."

They said nothing as I got in and started the engine.

I pulled out of the drive, began to round a corner. In the rearview, I saw Ethel rush toward the box.

2

—————

I drove long and winding roads that wove The Machine and me through rows of oaks and loblollies, paying only scant attention to my quarry. No doubt Harwood would've been his angel, his deliverer. But I'd prayed on it beforehand. For this human garbage, there'd be no easy way out.

Despite the trouble I'd gotten into back in Garth, I'd always respected Harwood. His department was as sullied as any other in a high crime area during that period. He knew what had to be done but at the same time had tried to go by the book, as well as the sensible addenda he'd tacked on to the book. I'd been the same, which was why I gave up the badge while men and women whose actions were far worse than mine went on to decorated careers. Warrantless search and seizure was one thing; roughing up perps who were far from first-time offenders was on the same side of the fence; but hassling folks just because of the color of their skin or the country they were born in or because they lived in the wrong neighborhoods? That was bullshit. The foulest kind.

There are various shades of justice—and then there's darkness in which no light can survive.

All through those gray days, I was castigated, coaxed, nudged, and shoved—but I'd refused to go along to get along, couldn't stay behind the blue line. It was just as well. Despite having no military background, I found my way to a private company that assisted the government with special operations. I learned on the job and don't mind saying I was one hell of a quick learner. Never went overseas, but domestic combat presented its own special layers of hell, especially when pretty much everything had to be done under social camouflage. When the Heartland Security Agency was established, I applied, was accepted, and thought I'd found my forever work home. But issues arose. Seems someone determined I was a little too *something* for their la-di-da unit of Peacemakers. Yet some higher-ups thought I'd be a good fit for one of their various off-the-books units. And I was—exceptionally—until I wasn't. Administration change and all that political bullshit. Same old tired folk song. But I'd played enough and knew enough rules to sing my own song. A nice little lullaby that I liked to call "Dead Sammie's Farm." I was gonna work it—but *my* way, in the dark, and with the assistance of some influential but in-the-day-shadows men and women who appreciated my work and had access to all kinds of resources. Black-ops venture capitalists.

My business now was tracking and ending the American Heartland's plague of deviants, the running-wilds infected with the White Fire Virus. Couldn't do it twenty-four seven, though. Every now and then I needed to take a break, relax my mind with a hobby: tracking fugitives and righting the wrongs of blind justice. "Shakes" had been a pleasant diversion. And yet deviants could be anywhere, could pop up at any time. It was about an hour's drive to get back home. Whenever I ventured away from the house, the closer I got when returning, the more I expected to see one dart out into the road in front of The Machine, challenging me. More of a wish, I admit, than an actual fear. Most often, I just saw woodland creatures—squirrels and other furry nutheads— risking their lives to forage for food. As I steered The Machine round a corner now, I saw something else: *more nutheads.*

Neglecting a rabbit and a stray whatever, my eyes went immediately to the olive van parked about half a mile from my driveway and the two frustrated-looking fools standing next to it. I shook my head, then chuckled. I'd need to talk to these two about a new MO. The broken-down-vehicle bit was getting a little tired. Admittedly, I enjoyed their shtick at first. If it was early in the morning, they made themselves up like easygoing sixty-somethings on their way to a farmers market or to the lake for a little fishing. Late at night, a middle-aged couple on their way home from a banquet or classy nightclub. Middle of the day brought the biggest range of light disguises—today it was a youngish and dopey husband and wife who seemed befuddled by two flat tires. I suppose their story to any Samaritans other than myself would be that they'd already called road service and were just waiting. I was genuinely surprised they'd been able to pull it off for so long, even if their visits were few and far between and, each time, they used a different vehicle. Sooner or later, though, the wrong vehicle filled with the wrong sort would turn the corner, roll down the window, spot these two clowns, and blast them, either suspecting something was up with them or, hell, just for fun.

Schupbach and Watton. Not really husband and wife, though I knew something was going on with them. Officially they were analysts with the bland-sounding Regional Climate Monitor Agency. Unofficially they were so far off the books no auditor would ever even blink, let alone think to call "foul." They were one of the knots in my tether to the HSA core, two among the elite crew of my deep, dark liaisons. They'd arrived in a van suitable for transporting prisoners. *Wonder who they were here for . . .*

I pulled over to the side and parked a few yards behind them. Out of The Machine, I locked it and let the smart minitank further secure itself with a repel field as I approached the two: both tanned, undoubtedly armed, and more than skilled at various hand-to-hand techniques. Watton, a lean, sinewy woman with a chestnut bob, was squatting next to the tire. Schupbach leaned over her, mumbling. He was a beefy guy with acorn hair, cut and styled in a classic crew. Their easygoing postures were betrayed by their tense jaws and hard gazes, fixed on the car while they positioned themselves and used their ears to "watch" my approach. In turn, I used my specs to get a better view of the surroundings.

The specs appeared very much like sports goggles to observers, their lenses tinted with a faint shade of greenish-orange; but they gave me a very clear view, like prescription glasses. Better, they could be adjusted to enhance my vision in a wide variety of ways. They helped me see through illusions; they helped me detect the invisibles. Presently, I saw nothing out of the ordinary—other than my not-so-welcome handlers.

I smiled as I neared, affected a southern Georgia drawl as I asked, "Y'all need some help?"

Schupbach straightened as he pretended to just now notice me. "Could use some, buddy." He grinned like an idiot man-child. "You know how to change a tire?"

"I know how to change a tune," I said when close enough so my voice wouldn't carry. "Do you realize how ridiculous you two look? You're askin' for trouble."

"And we heard you already found some," Schupbach said.

I smiled. "Good news travels fast, huh?"

Watton nodded over my shoulder toward The Machine. "Want to turn over your package to us?"

They had to be kidding. "You can have what's left after the victim's survivors have their final say."

She sighed. "Come on now, Frank. This guy—Elroy—he's not even a carrier. Not within the parameters of your ink-spotted jurisdiction."

"He's a runner," I said. "A fugitive from justice. He's within *every* law enforcement authority's jurisdiction."

Schupbach began, "You don't have a badge—"

I hardened my gaze. "Don't need one for a raper of kids."

He closed his mouth then opened it again, looking like he wanted to jab back. I blocked and counterpunched, shifting my gaze between the both of them as I said, "The HSA is dedicated to, among other things, protecting the sanctity of American families—correct?" Both of them shied away from my gaze, pretending to check for eavesdroppers among the trees. "*Correct*," I said. "So then now how did you fine folks miss this one for ten long years?"

Watton said, "We can't let you just"—she looked about and got a bit more careful—"*dispose* of him."

"You don't need to *let* me do anything."

"*Frank…*"

"I don't ask for permission for my retirement hobby. No sane man would."

Schupbach began, "Let's make a deal—"

"*No*." These fools were wasting my time. I needed to get

this bum secured and tucked away in the underground chapel, then wash up in time to pick Frankie up from school. I didn't want to be the last parent there again. Not three days in a row.

"Listen," said Schupbach, "we promise we'll handle this guy."

"You know we're not going to let him back out on the street," Watton said.

"I don't know anything." These secret lovers had never out-and-out steered me wrong before—if they had, we wouldn't even have been having this conversation. But I'd only had a handful of *meets* with them, enough to know they had their own shaded versions of truth. They were subservient to Unc Sam, just as I had once been. What else could I expect with them or any of my other "knots"? A casual conversation with them could be like bartering with black-market fishmongers. But I didn't have all day. I gave in just a little. "What do you want?"

"There's some trouble up across the border. In Postille, Virginia."

"Oh really?" I widened my eyes but refrained from waving my arms. "*Virginia?* The land running thick with alphabet soup? Home base of the CIA, HSA, and all other sorts of outfits even I don't know about? Not to mention more private contractors than I can count—"

Schupbach raised his hands in mock surrender. "They all have more trouble than they can keep track of these days."

"And this job in particular requires your expertise," Watton added. "Anyway, the potential trouble area is just across the border, closer to us than the DC area. More our problem than theirs."

"The Man wants you to head up there ASAP," Schupbach said.

I crossed my arms. "Is the Man going to head over to the school, pick up my little girl, feed and look after her while I'm gone?"

"Arrangements will be made, Frank. You know that." Schupbach glanced toward The Machine. "We've always got your back."

I narrowed my eyes.

"Listen, is there somewhere more secure we can talk?" Watton scanned the tall, reaching trees more intensely this time. "Being outdoors and all . . ."

Even if we hadn't been keeping our voices down, I wasn't worried. My property was wired to pick up anything amiss within a healthy radius—like, say, any *better* spies who might be lurking in the surrounding woods. This included anything with less than four legs and that wasn't on or near the road. We were well within the radius, and my watch would've tickled my pulse if any of the surveillance gadgets had picked up anything that might not be kosher. The HSA in conjunction with some bright-boy contractors had set up the entire system, and it hadn't failed me yet. Though now I looked over both shoulders—just for show—and nodded. "All right. Fix your damn tires and follow me in."

I meandered back to The Machine. I even took time once there to check on my prisoner. He'd pissed himself. Shitted too. Got some of the mess on the tarp I'd laid under him for just such an eventuality. I *tsked* him, then said, "It's only your waste coming out. Not your brains or intestines— though with you it's all the same, right? Hope you're still thinkin' about the choices you've made in life, shithead. We'll have confession later." I ignored whatever he tried to articulate through his gag, got in the driver's seat, and continued on my way to the house.

Schupbach and Watton could've worked the crew at a NASCAR race; they'd changed both tires and were raring to go by the time I passed them. They stayed close behind as I pulled into the lengthy driveway that led to an unassuming Tudor, loved and paid for by my late wife, fortified and secured by me and some trusted associates.

I pushed all the right buttons, punching in all the necessary codes to ensure that my security system recognized and allowed two and only two vehicles on the premises. I parked just outside the garage, secured my vehicle, and waited for my guests to do the same. I then escorted them through the front door and into the living room. I gestured with two fingers and a wave toward the leather sectional—my polite invite for them to park their asses.

"You two thirsty?"

"What are you offering?" Schupbach asked.

"Bottled water and ice tea, also in a bottle."

"Brand?" Watton asked.

I stopped halfway to the kitchen. "What?"

"Of the water." She crossed her legs and leaned back. "Not in the mood for tea . . . But *60 Minutes* recently did a segment on bottled water, and—"

"You're drinkin' from the damn faucet." I continued into the kitchen, prepared them both a generous glass of ice water (straight from the faucet filter), and returned to the living room. I wasn't thirsty.

The two were sitting right next to each other in the middle, a slightly respectable space between them, equidistant from the glider recliner on one end and the reclining loveseat on the other. Rather than play their butler, I set the glasses on the travertine cocktail table two feet in front of them. They'd have to make an effort if they wanted to quench any thirsts.

"All right," I said as Watton scooched to the edge of her seat to grab both glasses, "what type of trouble are we talking about?"

Watton scrunched up her face, no doubt picking up traces of chlorine, as her partner sipped, swallowed, and responded. "Infinite Definite."

I exhaled, and took my time with it. Damned terrorists. "What else is new?"

"This crew." Watton placed her glass back on the table. "They usually operate in cells of two people—"

"They're not '*people.*'"

Watton took note of my flaring nostrils. She swallowed air and said, "You know what I mean, Frank."

I wasn't in the mood to debate science. "Get on with it."

"This cell is made up of a family of four. An actual household."

"*So?* Lock them in the damned house and burn it down."

"Yeah." Schupbach lowered his head, scratched his left temple with his forefinger. "Thought of that and similar actions. But see, they're a bit craftier than the average viral terrorists."

"How so?"

"The head of the family is . . . *was* one of our own. Former agent. Former Peacemaker. Someone you served with—in the *dark.*"

My neck muscles tensed. "Who?"

"Marcus Graham."

My heart raced. "*Graham?*" I remembered him as a good man. One hell of a formidable agent.

"Current Peacemakers have tried and failed against them," Watton said. "And time is slipping ever more quickly toward the tipping point. Word is, the family is threatening to wage some kind of war on a town. And they have partisans. The viral kind. And as I said, things around DC are intensifying. Agents around there already have their hands full. Without a specialist, the only way to take them out would be to decimate a neighborhood, or worse. All responsible parties concerned would like to avoid that kind of mess."

No doubt. "What about this family of his?"

Schupbach's face tightened, erasing all traces of any expression. "You'll be briefed if you accept."

"And if I don't?"

"Why wouldn't you?" Watton gazed at me with kitten eyes, all innocent. "It's right up your alley."

They knew me well. I cocked my head and nodded. "All right. Who's going to brief me?"

"Here." Her face still impassive, Watton reached into her handbag and pulled out a CD jewel box as she stood. She handed it to me as if it were a summons. Inside was a circular, golden disk. "We hear you got one hell of a player in that urban tank of yours."

That, I did. The Machine and my house's security system were among the most valuable resources provided to me by those who valued my work and the ideas fueling it. Part of my retirement package. Being a respected renegade had its perks. The most recent perk was a brand-new in-vehicle laptop.

I stood, weighing the box in my right hand. The pair couldn't say much more—that is, not much more that would be relevant. Now that I'd accepted the mission, all I needed to know would be on the disk. They turned toward the door. I followed to see them out. Watton put her hand on the knob. Schupbach paused. Both turned their heads halfway in my direction.

"Frank?"

"Yeah?"

"Your package?"

Their heads completed the turn. Both of them gazed at me expectantly. My upper lip curled. It was rare for them to care about my hobby. When they mentioned it at all, it was usually only in passing. Rather than give the usual dismissal, I played a hunch and hoped I was wrong. "Who the hell is the guy to you? The world would be better off without him."

They exchanged glances before returning their gazes to me; Schupbach's sharpened to a steel edge. "He's one of the outfit's assets."

"Above our pay grade, Frank," Watton added.

No, I wasn't wrong. Just disgusted. Another reason among many I wanted no clean ties to Sam. There was no such thing as "clean" with Washington.

"Just keep him on ice for a bit." I followed the two outside. "I may want one last good look at him when I return."

3

I had my "assurances" that Frankie would be looked after while I was gone—but I didn't want to place her in the hands of the dismal duo. I didn't fully trust them with Elroy, and I sure as hell wasn't going to put my little girl in their care too. Instead, I placed a call. Cordero—one of my partners for life—would pick her up. I had a quick chat with him to make sure all was kosher. Frankie was familiar with him and his family. Better, Cordero had a little girl roughly the same age who could keep her decent company till I returned. I gave him the usual shit about making sure to treat her like a princess without making her feel like one, but Cordero was a good man. *Trusted.* He knew how to handle my girl. His family was on the short list of those I wanted to adopt Frankie if and when something ever happened to me. This mission, which was as chancy as some of the others I'd been on lately, could be it.

After a power nap, I gave The Machine a sanitizing more thorough than a juice cleanse, then packed everything I thought I might need into it. I even packed some stuff I hoped I wouldn't need—but one never knew.

I freshened up but didn't get suited up. I went only halfway there, gearing myself up in durable jeans, comfortable boots, and a reinforced long-sleeve shirt. I exchanged the stocked tactical vest with the tactical-scenario vest and filled the gun holster with my go-to carry: a Sig Sauer P320. I double-checked my inventory, checked the time, then turned on the laptop on the docking station in between The Machine's driver's and front passenger's seats. The first thing I saw was the oath.

I swear on the Promise of the Lord God and Mother Nature to always strive to maintain divine balance while pushing humankind to transcend its own skin and become Born Again, worthy caretakers of Creation and messengers to its creatures, discovered and undiscovered; in this temporal struggle, I have chosen my side, a deliverer of the true, fair, and living Paradise, one secure in the knowledge that the war shall only be won by eradicating nihilists in whatever form, environment, or circumstance in which I may find them. If I should fall, my blood, provided by God, is destined to be spilled, given to the Earth, and used to nourish the souls growing the sustenance for the angels to come.

Most hunters swore to some variation if not those exact words. To be honest, the vast majority of hunters kept it short and sweet, beginning with "eradicating" and ending with "nihilists," which was all well and good with me. But in my more reflective moments, I recalled the oath, remembering why I lived the life I lived. We humans weren't meant for death. We were meant for something greater. But those who stood in the way of humankind's destiny . . . Well, when dealing with them, the concept of "transcending the skin" took on a new meaning.

The words stayed on-screen long enough for me to skim them twice before the computer finished booting up. I then checked for messages that might've been sent but for whatever reason didn't make it to my smartphone. There were none. All redundant. I sent out an Orange alert—our little hunting club's version of such—to three confederates I wanted for this outing. Finally, I hit the road, waiting till I got to the last stoplight before the highway to put on my headphones and slide the disk in the player. The wizards at the HSA (with, as always, the strong assistance of their equally brilliant contractors) had developed a neat little program that not only conveyed all the info I needed in code but also entwined those codes with unique and useful little subliminals: *When in the field, if the enemy does so-and-so, you do such-and-such.* This was all highly experimental, of course. It was still being tested under highly controlled conditions. But off-the-books operatives like yours truly had the opportunity to test it in the field. And I was happy to do so, despite the high potential for irreparable brain scrambling.

Getting what I needed, I took off the headphones and turned to one of my playsets on the radio, letting Waylon croon and play, relaxing my mind and body, getting ready.

Waylon had begun talking about Clyde and his electric bass when The Machine carried me across the Virginia border at about an hour before midnight. Within a minute of crossing, I sent out another coded message to the three confederates. Raker hit me back, sending me coordinates on where we would all meet and when. I punched them into my GPS. The meeting place was thirty to forty-five minutes away. The meeting time was in ninety minutes. I switched the playlist to Shooter Jennings and poured on the gas. I wanted as much time as possible to check out the place before anyone arrived. More than once, a local cop car took heed and followed me—none of them for more than three minutes before begging off. Not even the state police. All Virginia cops, it seemed, recognized the tags on my plates—they were nonsense to the average citizen, but to anyone with any authority, they meant *Mind your own damned business unless you want to be a customer of the boys and girls backing me.*

The tags saved me a lot of time and trouble if not nasty looks. In this day and age, vehicles the size of mine were viewed as an annoyance on civilian roads. My particular modified transport was viewed as nothing less than an intrusion—just as I damn well wanted it to be. We Americans were involved in a domestic war, even if most citizens purposefully didn't realize it; I wanted *all* to be on edge so that no one was too shocked when all hell broke loose. But in my forced retirement—my "special" status—I had to make compromises. I couldn't go on the internet, publishing blogs screaming "holy hell"—nor could I run through the streets doing the same. And when it came to doing what I was so special at doing, it usually figured most of my targets were in secluded spots, away from too many public eyes. Unfortunately for my handlers, The ID had an aversion to reclusiveness.

Like something out of a generic comic about zombies or supervillains—or both—The Infinite Definite were an unorganized horde clamoring for the end of the world. Something beyond—another realm—was urging them to push our world *into* that beyond, that other realm, either by remaking our world in their image or by destroying it. Long ago, some government smarts came up with a shorter tag for the terrorists—"The ID," pronounced like and a reference to the *id*, the part of the human mind that is totally unconscious and serves as the source of instinctual impulses and demands for immediate satisfaction of primitive needs.

With their fantastic abilities, affiliates of The Infinite Definite considered themselves *more* than human despite committing acts that proved the opposite. Many of us fighting these bastards figured that "The ID" may as well have been short for either "idiosyncratic," as in the group's behavior, or "identification," as in the sudden and frequent changes in their appearance.

Graham's persona apparently hadn't changed too much, as they knew it was he who was committing acts that were the calling card of this loose cult of deviants. I guessed that was both good and bad: good in that he might be able to be reasoned with rather than snuffed out. But if he had truly fallen in with these inhuman bastards, if he truly believed that he was "chosen" to be a dark light unto humanity, exposing his deepest inner nature by committing sexually violent acts in order to convert or kill, then he had to be extinguished. Humankind's destiny was angelhood, not the opposite.

Within the vicinity of the warehouse, I parked in a secluded spot. Once outside of the vehicle, I locked it and set the hide-and-repel field with a few pushes of my key chain's buttons. The Machine was now secure and invisible to all but the most talented observers.

I had no idea about the dangers in this territory, but I still wasn't about to suit up. There was no need. My vest carried enough goodies for any off-season trick-or-treaters. And my specs would help ensure I saw the menaces in plenty of time, no matter what light tricks they used to conceal themselves. My hands were gloved up but free and ready, and my boots were truly made for stompin'. At the moment, they carried me softly down a dirt path as I adjusted my specs to detect both breathing threats and surveillance cameras. Nearing the grounds, I kept to the perimeter, the shadows, and circled, steadily closing in, shifting my specs through every filter as I cased the place for cameras, guards, loiterers, and anything else that might give me trouble. I circled maybe three times before I came within an arm's reach of the structure's walls. Satisfied I hadn't been made, I inched my way to the least conspicuous side door and, without much trouble, unlocked it. I wasn't worried about an alarm. Raker would've seen that it was disabled. That was part of the deal. The man who set the meeting location took care of the alarms and anything else he could. But we couldn't expect him to handle all security guards, late workers, or surprise drop-ins all by himself.

The interior was dusty, dark—but safe. After a quick adjustment, my specs dealt sufficiently with the darkness; I altered the rhythm of my breathing to prevent sneezing. In spite of my precautions—"*Snap!*"—Raker got the drop on me, coming up from behind and flicking me on the back of the head. He jumped back and wove beautifully out of the way of my counterattack as I quickly thrust back my foot and left elbow, following up with a turn and kick while going for the P320 with my right hand. I didn't touch the gun or even the holster. I'd recognized the voice and managed to prevent all my reflexes from completing their cycle.

Raker stood in the dim light, grinning silently. He wasn't quite as big as a bull, but the dusky man could hit like one. Thankfully, he sported a flattop instead of horns. His look hadn't changed one bit from a few months ago. Back then, though, he was down in my territory, helping me subdue a gang of Fire-Virals who'd organized themselves into a deranged version of a football team. They were rampaging through a neighborhood, trampling, tackling, and tearing apart anyone they saw, especially pregnant women, whose fetuses they ripped out and passed like footballs, occasionally punting them. There was no damned sense to any of it but over-the-top terror. Proof positive that these deviants lacked souls. I'd never had much talent for organized sports; Raker had been All-Pro during his brief stint as a professional football player before joining the HSA and failing a bid for state assembly. He, chief among others, had helped me eliminate all eleven of the deviants; naturally, he was the first one I thought of when rolling onto his territory, where another group was threatening to engage in similar activities.

"Raker."

"Sanders . . . my *man*."

We shook hands briefly, then hugged for a bit longer.

"How's tricks?" I asked.

"*Solid*, not shady."

I chuckled. "Yeah, sure."

I followed Raker into a wider area with high rows of crates on one side and forklifts on the other. In front of us was the loading area. The garage doors were shut, separating us from the big trucks on the other side. It was the area with the best lighting and the most room to maneuver. After I'd gotten a good 360-degree look, Raker faced me; his expression had done away with all pretense of pleasure at our reunion. He cleared his throat. "I gotta say, when I got your call, it sparked something in my head. There's something you and I need to rap about."

I began to ask for elaboration but was interrupted by a side door opening and a booming Latin-tinged voice announcing, "*Brothers! Arms!*"

In his late twenties, Juliano Castro was the youngest of the confederates I'd assembled. His youth carried pluses and minuses. He'd entered the side door with a swagger, his arms stretched wide and his words obviously taking on a double meaning, as he intended to hug us both while he was already halfway decked out in hunting gear. I had no problem obliging; I knew how to hug safely. I just wished he weren't so strident when it came to volume. At this time of night, in this type of environment, voices could carry.

I whispered when my lips were an inch away from his ear, "Keep it low, bro."

After the brotherly greetings were through, Juliano asked, "So what's so urgent? We got another sprinter off the path?"

"Yeah, I'd heard about this Graham," Raker said. "But from back in the day. Only rumors. What's he gotten into?"

I parted my lips to answer, then twitched, sensing movement to my right. We all turned, each reaching for our personal favorite among our midrange accessories—my choice was a vamper—before we, in unison, relaxed upon seeing that bright-red patch of hair where the dye looked like it had been dropped from a good height to splatter smack dab in the middle of an otherwise ink-black 'do. "Sorry I'm late, boys"—she had a voice like molten asphalt —"but I come bearing sweets." Krissy Morgan emerged from the shadows. Her weapons remained holstered or hidden. She carried a tablet in her left hand.

Juliano perked up once he got a good look. "You always do, cupcakes."

She glared at him. "I meant in my head, jackass. Got a bead on the fam."

I straightened. "What do you mean?"

"Hun, you gave me a peppery name and some hinty pieces. I ran the damned meat through every slaughter-house database I knew. Marcus Graham: former Fed, family man, possibly troubled, definite troublemaker . . . Not hard, boys. Marcus Graham is no longer 'Marcus Graham.' He's changed names a few times since then. Certainly a family man—probably listens to Hall and Oates every morning."

Raker shook his head. "Girl, what are you talking about?"

"He wants to be *left alone*, Pharis." She swatted at the air. "Get up on the music you grew up with."

Raker looked about to defend his dinged pride when I said, "Get to the point. About Graham or whatever he's going by now."

"Well"—her eyes fell toward her tablet's screen—"our friend has moved quite a bit since he's fallen out of favor."

"Your databases or other resources tell you why?" Juliano asked.

"Former agents tend to be shady types. Paranoid and/or up to no good." She met my eyes and smiled.

I smiled back, less at her implication and more out of being impressed at what she'd found in such a limited time.

"He's holed up in a cabin," she continued. "One of our designated safe cabins."

"That's a little on the nose," I said.

"Yeah, well, he's made himself nice and comfortable. He doesn't leave it much," Krissy said. "Nighttime is the right time to hit him. Predawn is best."

As I'd pretty much already figured. The deviants kept to out-of-the-way places—woodlands and other familiar locales of horrific, too-grim fairy tales—until their lusts grew too strong to let them stay put. As far as nighttime being the right time, it usually was. Darkness was our friend. Lack of light, a deviant's enemy.

Staid and serious, Raker turned toward me. "What do you know?"

We were all standing close now, no more than five feet

from one another. They were rapt, ready to hang on my words. I took a breath, sat on a small stack of cinder blocks, then ran it all down.

"Marcus Graham—or whatever he's calling himself these days—is the head of a family of four. All four individuals are infected with the White Fire Virus. Rather than turn themselves in to be quarantined—or even report themselves to the appropriate doctors so they may take the appropriate medications to neuter their abilities—they try to live like a normal family. Too normal. Despite what Krissy's intel has told her—which, by the way, I don't fully doubt—mine tells me they often make points of mingling with the community. Making friends. Visiting and allowing visitors. Worst of all, they host dinner parties. Get-togethers. Great way of introducing themselves to the neighborhood. And it's at these events that they infect their guests. Get 'em drunk or drugged and proceed with the orgy."

There were the expected aghast expressions to go along with the unexpected silence. I thought at least Juliano would have a comment—but no. So I continued.

"Then they move on. Every three or so months."

"That seems . . ." There was Juliano, searching for words.

Raker found them. "A bit more of a sophisticated method than what The ID usually employs."

Krissy shook her head. "Not really. Most fancy themselves as artists. Hosting events—dinners, barbeques, what have you—that *is* a form of art."

"But," said Juliano, "to pass themselves off as normal, enough to be accepted over a period of time—that's a little out of the ordinary."

I nodded my agreement. "That's probably why I was told to reach out and make the final contact. They're good at blending; they're good at disappearing and remaking themselves. Good enough to fool the everyday Peacemakers, the clean boys and girls who go through all the right and proper channels. Well, those boys and girls have tried and failed because they didn't understand the etiquette."

"And you needed the three of us?" Raker asked. "Sounds like something you'd want to handle alone or with a one-partner limit."

Krissy narrowed her eyes at me. "You know more. A *lot* more."

"Yeah," said Juliano, "what's up? Who is this guy really?"

I raised an eyebrow at the young'n. "I can tell you *what* he was. One hell of a gangbuster."

"So were a lot of Peacemakers," Krissy said.

I shook my head. "Graham was different. No banger intimidated him."

"That's every Peacemaker worth her salt," Krissy piled on.

I took a deep breath and let it out with a sigh as my shoulders slumped. "Back you-know-when, Graham and I were on special assignment. An op so hush-hush even some members of our own nonexistent unit were kept in the dark about it. There were some crews who were making a bid to become the most notorious gang on the West Coast. They took Asian and Middle Eastern criminal organizations as their models. There was one banger in particular—Russel Z.—also known as 'Ruzz.' Known as an all-around badass. But really a mama's boy, even if he rarely saw her growing up. We knew this, so we rounded up all the sleazes who'd ever slept with his mama, trussed 'em up, and put them in a big room—some warehouse near some river. Then we collared the punk, restrained his wrists and ankles, and steered him to the room filled with all of them. He was a tough guy till we did the introductions and told him these dirty assholes all screwed his mother. He wasn't such a tough guy then; tough guys' eyes don't well up over what's long passed. Graham, not wasting a plum second, gave the fool an option: the banger could either split their skulls open right then and there, or we would do it for him. Before the punk could answer, Graham went down the row, naming each man, running down their sexual history and, more specifically, their adventures with the punk's mother. One of them—a man Graham refused to single out—was Russel's biological father. *All* of them, though, had treated her like shit—worse than a dog. Some of them had even literally shit on her—or so Graham had said, giving choice details. Not that any of us had reason to doubt him. But he didn't stop there. Graham went on to tell the shithead how many half siblings he had 'cause of his deadbeat father's further misadventures."

My confederates were aghast—again. Not a good sign. I hadn't even gotten to the worst of it. I hoped they could stand this. If not, they wouldn't be ready for this battle.

"Graham emphasized to the would-be gang lord how he had all these half brothers and half sisters runnin' around and knew none of them—none of them except for one. Another young punk by the name of Lonston, known in the streets as 'Longstrong.' Ruzz knew that name well. It was the handle of another banger on the rise. His numero-uno rival. When the kid's jaw dropped—and, honestly, some of ours did too—Graham left the room. He returned less than a minute later, pushing Longstrong himself, gagged and bound in a chair like the others. He went into another room and delivered another person: Ruzz's mother. Gagged and bound. Graham was in his own zone now. It was his show. The rest of us were the bit players. We listened and said nada. And from that point on, Graham spoke primarily through action. He approached Ruzz with two carry cases, opened them in front of him, and—as he freed his feet and hands—offered him his choice of weapon."

Raker's nostrils flared. "The hell was the point of all this?" he growled.

Krissy shook her head. "Frank, you didn't try to step in?"

I narrowed my gaze at her. "None of us did. As I said, it was his show. We were just there to keep everyone and everything in check till it reached Marc's desired end. The point was to reach down to the wisp of a soul that Ruzz had left, get a hold of it, and give the banger a chance to recognize it, rescue it, work to redouble it, solidify it—or just blow it all away, once and for all."

Raker and Krissy exchanged glances as Juliano asked, almost breathlessly, "What happened?"

I shrugged. "Ruzz chose the PMR-30 in the left case. He kissed his mother on the cheek, locked eyes with Longstrong, and then raised the gun, turned, and fired. One philandering man dead, shot between the eyes. Then another, same way. On down the line, till all of them fell."

"He no doubt had some rounds left over," Raker said quietly. "Graham wasn't worried the punk would take a shot at him?"

I shook my head. "We had more than half a dozen guns trained on 'im, and Graham was armored up. We all were. Kid was smart enough to know we'd drop him before he could make good, then his whole life would've been for nothing. Instead he, his mother, and his half brother lived. Together they worked with the HSA to help keep a good portion of West Coast gangland under control. Graham, Ruzz, and mom, the three grew to be like family from what I heard. A long-distance family anyway. But Graham was loyal; he kept in touch. Shortly after that incident, though . . . Well, I lost touch with Graham."

"Wow." Juliano rubbed the back of his neck. "Okay."

Krissy straightened her posture and lifted her chin. "So the takeaway here is that he's big on family and uses it to achieve his version of order. Real family, fake family—"

"Symbolize all you want," I said. "My point is that you need to be ready for *anything* with him. I don't know what type of man or whatever he is now, and I hope to have a good chat with him. But if I don't get that chance, you need to be ready to take him and his out. *Quickly*. Without blinking."

I met each of their eyes as I stood, and they met mine. No flinching, no blinking, no slumped shoulders as I now stood straight, having an advantage in height over most of them. Their jaws were tight, their chests puffed, and they now looked like I'd remembered each of them from the last time we'd separately met. They'd swallowed everything I'd just told them, and though it wasn't tasty, they'd digested it quickly. *That's* why they were among the most trusted of my confederates. They were among the best. Too extreme for a federal agency—but not so for a few benefactors at the core.

"All right," Raker said, "we got the house. We know the target. Everything's in the vicinity."

"We're doing this tonight, huh?" Juliano's voice didn't crack, and he looked as steady as he had a moment before, but that shouldn't even have been a question.

I responded in a measured tone, "If you all are ready, I've got everything I need. And like Krissy said, three to four a.m. is peak strike time, especially for these alleged 'normal' types. They're most likely in bed."

"The plan?" Raker asked.

"Seek to subdue. I want an audience with Graham. But I

don't want a wrestling match with any of them. Permanently subdue any who won't listen to reason."

Krissy swallowed just a tad too emphatically. She didn't want to go against me, but I didn't want hesitaters out in the field with me. "Yeah, Krissy? Question?"

"Not a regular gang, Frank. We're talking a family. The kids haven't even neared puberty."

"The kids?" Juliano spat out a broken chuckle. "They're the most dangerous! Remember Paley County?"

"Those were *teenagers*," Krissy said through clenched teeth.

"Yeah"—Raker nodded—"no doubt about PC. I don't recall ever seeing turned kids younger than ten, or even hearing about such carriers." He raised an eyebrow in my direction. "Kill them all, Frank?"

Krissy lowered her chin a bit toward her chest but kept her eyes on me. "*Your* call. Capture the kids?" The look in her eye told me she questioned my judgment in this area. She shouldn't have; she knew about Frankie. And Krissy's judgment, I respected. But I was the only one who knew Graham.

"Let's play it by ear." I chose the middle way. "Now let's circle up."

We tightened the spaces between us, reaching for one another's hands. Raker quietly led us in prayer. Then we all went silent, continuing to pray inwardly on our own. Each of us came from slightly different faith traditions, but we all essentially prayed for the same thing—or so I hoped.

4

———

As nimble a researcher as she was and as good as her resources seemed to be, Krissy hadn't been able to procure a detailed layout of the house. It was ironic, considering it was one of our hunting club's safe cabins, but it wasn't totally surprising. The cabins were to be used by traveling hunters who needed to stay off the grid while resting and replenishing. This particular cabin hadn't been used by any of our usual contacts, at least none of the ones we could reach at this hour. We'd be heading into unknown territory. Sure, we could've waited until the next night, as Juliano and, hell, maybe even Krissy seemed to want, but we then stood a greater chance of losing the target. When it came to deviants, I didn't like waiting. Plus, the local weather called for clear skies—always a good sign—as if the heavens themselves were on our side.

Krissy selected the secondary meet-up point, and we agreed on a time to get there and get dressed. Unlike Juliano, most of us had left the majority of our gear in our respective vehicles—but all of us had parked wisely. Before taking off, we all confirmed with one another that no one's vehicle had been disturbed.

Even though we had the GPS coordinates for the staging location, we let Krissy take the lead in getting us there. After weaving through several miles of nearly deserted roads lined with bitternut, pignut, and mockernut hickories—among a variety of other common Virginia trees—she signaled and pulled us off-road to weave deeper into the forest. Mucking our all-terrain tires on gravel and mud, we weren't exactly off the beaten path, but it was one most likely taken many times by hunters and fishermen who liked to get in a little practice during the off-season. It kind of seemed appropriate for us.

We entered a wide, tire-worn lot, and Krissy parked her armored SUV right at the blurred edge, next to a dense cluster of trees. The rest of us found our own best spots and secured our vehicles after exiting them. I checked our surroundings, adjusting my specs to detect anything I could with them that I couldn't with normal twenty-twenty human sight.

We circled up again—but not to pray. The time for appeals was long over.

"On foot from here?" Juliano asked.

Krissy nodded. "Best way to get there."

"And the best way to catch them unawares," Raker said.

Krissy pulled up a map of the woods on her phone and showed us approximately where we were headed. "We can set coordinates after we get dressed."

I nodded. "Then let's suit up."

Juliano kept a lookout, checking the perimeter, while the rest of us got our gear. I always carried two suits in The Machine, a luxury most other hunters couldn't afford. Because I'd worked my way up, getting in good with the right people by doing the right deeds, the right and necessary supplies were rarely a problem for me. My only problem was trying to determine what accessories to carry out into the field. The vest and belt would only bear so much before they became a burden, and it was usually wise to keep the backpack light. First things first: I switched out my specs for prescription "reading" glasses, which were designed to sync perfectly with my helmet's visor.

Deviants could manipulate electromagnetic radiation—a large range of light. They could also be *painfully* manipulated by it, so much so that they tore themselves apart, or desperately tried to, in order to end the suffering brought on by too much or too skillfully directed exposure. So a deviant-hunter's gear was a bit different from that of the average cop, hunter, or soldier.

The battle-dress uniforms had been designed by government contractors even darker than us hunters, for original purposes that may as well have been classified in concrete. The silver-and-gold uniforms were essentially glorified hazmat suits, though the hazardous materials we faced were mostly from some section of the beautiful, deadly electromagnetic spectrum. They were also custom-designed and, consequently, far more exoskeletal than the baggy sort that above-ground professionals were used to. Forearm and shin protectors, as well as reinforcement in the elbow and knee areas, helped with hand-to-hand combat, though many of us had been trained to not let it come to that or had learned how to end it quickly when it did. The various accessories on our belts and in the pouches and holsters of the tactical-scenario vests that fit over the suits were designed to keep deviants more than an arm's length away. Our boots had composite toes, but our gloves weren't designed for fisticuffs. Our helmets could probably withstand more blows.

They were modeled to look a bit deviant themselves—half human skull, half Hollywood version of an alien. What appeared as a menacing rictus to an outside observer served triple duty as part respirator, voice changer, and telecom device that allowed a hunting party to communicate clearly with one another—helmet to helmet—on a frequency that would sound like meaningless garble to any eavesdropping deviants. The extended triangular filter over the nose worked with the rictus respirator (and vice versa) to parse certain gases and noxious odors in order to ensure relatively clean air. Buggy fly-eye visors allowed us to make clear and present sense of the invisible, the visually deranged, and the time-placement challenged—in daylight or darkness. Our "night vision" gave us the common green tint, but—in my case at least—the special sight could be adjusted to give me a clearer view; that was thanks in large part to the "reading" glasses I wore. The earholes could magnify sounds unheard by the common human ear and filter out the "common sounds" of whatever environment in which we happened to be hunting. In the woods, it could be adjusted to filter out insects and birds, though sometimes the winged creatures were good indicators of where true danger might be hiding.

Nothing was perfect, but my uniform had yet to completely fail me in a hostile situation, even if my successful hunts were most often hinged on my brainpower over any device. Nevertheless, for this outing, I smartly (I hoped) chose a couple of super-stunner grenades, some Skrapnel capsules, a telescopic baton, a spice canister, and a vamper. A gunlight was attached near the left shoulder of the tactical vest, where the radio normally would be, and then there were the real guns: a .50 caliber semiautomatic (holstered on my right thigh), a .44 Mag revolver (tucked in my vest's holster), and a Kel-Tec PMR-30 (holstered and stashed away in the backpack, just in case). Finally, I tossed a grab bag of goodies and wilderness survival accessories into my backpack, keeping it as light as possible. The other hunters would be making their own choices from a similar selection. Some would even choose longer-range guns, high-powered rifles and such—but that wasn't my style.

After we geared up, we more fully secured our vehicles, expanding the hide-and-repel fields. Then, forming a half circle around Krissy, we typed the target coordinates into the suits' wristbands. Among other things, the flat black bands acted as compasses. We didn't have to look at them as they synced up with our helmets and fed us signals to ensure we didn't stray too far from the goal.

I tested our telecom links, speaking each hunter's name and listening for the clear response. We made the necessary adjustments and went through the cycle of call-and-response until satisfied we'd be able to communicate easily with one another among the trees while being heard by no one else. We adjusted our helmets' visor settings to give us each our own most comfortable version of night vision. Then, two abreast, with Krissy and me in the lead, we entered the woods. "Keep the lines clear," I said, "except for necessary chatter. I'll do the roll calls every three minutes." No one said a word as we fanned out steadily among the pines, each of us taking a different pathway. We planned to converge on the cabin from four points, covering all sides.

Camping wasn't permitted in this forest. Of course there were always lawbreakers, nomads, reckless teenagers, and the like, but for the most part, we had little chance of happening upon innocent bystanders. The trees were predominantly pine. Even when I adjusted the visor settings, the trees didn't appear to change. They remained wood and bark and needles and cones of different ages.

Good. A hunter couldn't be too careful. Some affiliates of The ID were talented enough to manipulate more than light. They could manipulate their entire environment, creating what we called HotSpots. Otherworldly settings plucked from another dimension and plunked down in our world, under the full control of the Infinite Definite terrorist who'd brought it here. The suits were designed to help us maneuver those treacheries as well.

I did roll call, then went deeper. The forest got darker, the spaces between trees seemingly narrower. I adjusted the spectrum on my visor to cope, but it didn't help as much as I'd wished. Most trees, I made out just fine. But some were so black I thought I was staring into the void of space, seeing only a few pinpricks of distant stars.

I fiddled with the helmet's audial filters. That helped some with navigation. I heard the expected. The benefit of hunting at night was that there were fewer natural sounds to contend with—no birds other than the occasional owl, a few scurrying critters, and the usual nocturnal insects, not to mention the crunch of twigs and pine cones I just couldn't avoid treading over. My best aid in keeping me undeterred were the tiny sensors embedded in the suit at certain strategic points, perpetually sending out close-range sound waves; the responses ultimately hit the cartilage of my ears just right, making them tickle-tingle in response, a sign that the natural and hairlike sensors in my inner ear were helping me keep my balance, the suit and my reflexes working in unison to control the flow of my movements, keeping me from tripping over or banging into anything— and to prevent anything from getting the jump on me.

The result, though, was that I moved at the speed of a sloth. That was great overall for stealth—one minded one's movements and footfalls more—but it made it much more of a creep walk for me, and no doubt for my compatriots as well. I did roll call. All responded, with a few brief comments on the darkening paths. No complaints, though. These were professionals.

The farther I went, the trees remained mostly the same in appearance, but the bark of some displayed odd patches —a faint luminescent dusting no bigger than handprints, in size if not shape. In and of itself, this was not alarming. But even after fiddling with some of my helmet's settings, I saw no owls and heard no other night-creature sounds. Not a good sign. When deviants claimed a section of the environment, other animals tended to flee. And yet several yards in, deep among the trees, I detected no true signs of anything amiss and heard nothing of import from my confederates. I checked my left wristband and saw we were a little past the third three-minute mark. I did roll call.

"Nothing here," Raker responded.

"Ditto," Krissy said.

"Nada." Juliano was trying his best, but even over the channel, his voice wavered after less than fifteen minutes in.

Normally, I would've said nothing more. But after Juliano's word, I heard a sound I didn't recognize and didn't like—a clattering—as if someone were playing pitch-and-catch with a large sack full of silverware and broken porcelain. I had the fleeting thought that someone was on our link, communicating with us or just plain laughing at us. But the thought was gone with the sound.

"You all heard that?" I asked.

"What?"

"Heard what?"

"*¿Qué?*"

Three versions of the same response. I figured it was all my imagination, so I just said, "Stay sharp. We don't need—"

I stopped short as something clothed in silver and gold emerged from behind a tree no more than thirty feet in front of me. It was the same height as me, about the same build, and it was definitely wearing a similar uniform. But no backpack. It wasn't one of the others. He—I presumed it was a "he"—carried something in his left hand, something I didn't quite recognize, *couldn't*, as it made his entire hand glow. He approached me as cautiously as I did him. I debated speaking with a modulated voice—less of a debate was to have my hand at the ready to grab my revolver.

He suddenly raised his hand, and I saw a bright flash; the visor was no help at all, but my suit was. I didn't feel a thing. And when my vision cleared, the mystery hunter was gone. But everything around me seemed a bit wobbly.

I prepared to warn others about the rogue. A bestial scream cut me off. An avalanche of static flooded my eyes. *Shit*. The cabin wasn't even in proximity yet. We didn't need whatever the hell this was. My vision cleared as I adjusted my audials to filter out the noise. "*Status! Everyone!*" I tried not to sound panicked.

"Same position," Raker said. "Stable."

"Ditto!" Krissy said. "But—" *Garble*. A female's scream was lost in the snow of static.

"Raker!" I said. "Move to J's position. Narrate!"

"Copy!"

I double-timed toward Krissy's last position. The slight inclines and declines, embedded rocks, and root clumps all became more of a problem at this pace. But it was unavoidable; I didn't like what I was hearing. Industrial sounds. City sounds. Jackhammering. Vehicles crashing. Horns blowing. Blowtorches firing up. Heavy machinery pressing, clanging, self-destructing. Those were the images my mind formed anyway, all of them incongruous with my immediate environment, which was most likely the point. It didn't help that my visor, on its own, slid through a range of vision settings, attempting to slow me even further.

I could barely hear Raker's voice: "Soil . . . not soil . . . dusted . . . glowing . . . tracks . . . cones . . . *biting . . . Shit!*"

The city and factory noises all ran together now. As they got louder, they were almost unbearable. I couldn't hear Raker even if he was still speaking. The targets were on us; that much was clear. They'd broken our code and gotten onto our wavelength—*definitely* not good. I'd have to go dark.

I switched off the telecom link and set the visor to normal vision, which meant that above the shoulders I had the senses of a normal human, stumbling about in a post-midnight, predawn heavily wooded area. But here is where the suit's sensors really did their stuff. Thanks to a half-moonlit clear sky above, I wasn't engulfed in total darkness. Just to tilt the odds a bit more in my favor, I switched on the gunlight perched on my shoulder, using it for one of its intended uses: high-intensity flashlight.

Now, I was able to focus a little more on the terrain, keep better balance, and move much more quickly—but the environment had more surprises in store.

I smelled it first: rotting wood, followed by a decaying animal that was long dead, maybe several of them. The smell was strong enough to bypass my helmet's filters. Farther ahead, I saw what Raker had meant about the tracks and the cones. The conifers' discards were scurrying to and fro, having been converted into some kind of cross between armadillos and rats. More than a few of them were hostile. As I dutifully followed the fluorescent tracks that looked like human footprints, doing my best to avoid now-mobile cones, I inevitably came close to stepping on a few of the bastards; their reaction was to leap at me, jaws and claws at the ready. Attempting to sink their teeth into my uniform, they released a noxious odor. Whether it was part of a combination attack or just out of frustration that their teeth didn't penetrate, I didn't know, but the faintly visible clouds of stench managed to bypass my helmet's filter. I had no time to adjust the setting, but after the third attack by a converted cone, I knew I was close to where I was going.

I rounded two more trees, then saw them: a girl and a goat.

I unholstered my revolver, dimmed the gunlight, and adjusted my visor's setting.

The fair-haired girl was in pajamas, and barefoot. Her hands were free and unmoving. She was maybe five or six, no more than seven years old. Her pajamas were a two-piece set, possibly made of wool, and cream-colored with pink patterns that to my eyes looked like octopi. Her eyes were cast toward the ground, looking at all the coniferous critters. The light wasn't great here, but it didn't need to be for her kind. She no doubt had made me before I made her, yet she paid me no mind. Hunters' uniforms were designed to make it difficult for the deviants to look directly at us, but that wasn't the issue here. The glimpses I caught of her expression showed she was pleased about something, possibly about an accomplished conversion job on the environment. Her presence wasn't entirely unexpected, but no one had said anything about a goat.

An Arapawa goat, to be exact. It was a rare breed, so this goat probably wasn't all that it appeared to be. Mostly white but with black-and-fawn patterns, it had sweeping rather than backward-pointing horns, which meant it was a male. The average weight of a buck is about one hundred to one hundred twenty-five pounds. This one, while having adult features, was smaller, maybe half that weight. Red-eyed and leering, it was foaming at the mouth. The froth had a dark, pinkish hue. I wasn't so daft to assume that all it had was rabies.

Hell creature notwithstanding, the girl was the immediate threat, and I wanted a straight kill while I could get a clean shot. I was damn sure this was Graham's daughter—a deviant, not an illusion and not an innocent human. With the visor's assist, I detected signs of those damned parasites in her skin.

I aimed the .44 Mag at the dead center of her forehead, just above her nose. That should've been the beginning of the end of it. But *damn it*, we made eye contact right before I pulled the trigger.

She didn't get in my head (thank the helmet for that), but something about the glance made the entire environment shift as *she* shifted, dodging the bullet, the gun's report acting as thunder to accompany the sudden and massive snow shower. Exactly what I was trying to avoid. A spot had turned *hot*. The converted pine cones were the first sign of a spot warming; the onslaught of flakes, white and pink, were the full arrival.

There was no way to get a clean shot now—though I wasted a few seconds trying, weaving closer (or at least thinking I was getting closer) while trying to get a bead on the girl. She and the goat seemed unworried, so much so that they even seemed to be doing some sort of cryptic dance with each other, the goat on its hind legs, both of them prancing and retreating the steps, circling, bowing and dipping, flipping and somersaulting, all of it further disorienting to me, if not to them.

Maybe the whole routine was a partial illusion, like the snow. After all, rather than the stuff cooling the environment, I felt increasingly warm until my suit temp-corrected. My gear had its limits, though—and it was a relatively low threshold. Just another reason to put an end to all of this. But the snow was increasingly distracting. The flake's pinkish colors were like the flesh of cherries. Like the flesh of . . .

Shit. Maybe the girl *had* gotten into my head. A sexual, perverse distraction—*that's* what she wanted to put in my head. Maybe she wanted me to think she couldn't possibly get in my head through my helmet. Maybe she wanted me to think these thoughts were my own. Or maybe, *maybe* she wanted me to think—

Stop. It was a rabbit hole. I had to stop thinking about her and stop *her*.

Bullets were too dangerous a tactic now. Both the girl and the goat were increasingly camouflaged with the environment. And there was no telling when or if Raker or the others might wander onto the scene. Holstering my revolver, I hurriedly adjusted my visor settings and did what I could to close the distance, retrieving two Skrapnel capsules from one of my vest's pouches with one hand and keeping my other hand near the telescopic baton on my belt as I lunged for the girl. She skipped and wove out of reach, keeping the safe-for-her distance between us. The goat, however, no longer felt like dancing—or so I gathered when it lunged at me. Realizing how near it was, I swung my baton, extending it in midswing and landing a good *thwack* on the side of the damned beast's head. It tumbled into the snow but quickly regained its footing. It gained something else as well.

Wings. They seemed to peel off its flanks as if they'd been there all along, pressed close, only now revealing themselves as the creature geared up for another assault. The unfolding wings acquired a pinkish hue, as did the goat itself. The wings appeared leathery; the goat's hide, scaly, like a reptile's. Its eyes glowed brighter red; the horns on its head elongated as fine splinters peeled off their sides, multiplying the sharp danger. The clouds I saw emitting from its nose weren't condensed breath. They were darker, sootier —*smoke*.

The damned thing was no longer just a nuisance I could whack around; it was more like a miniature dragon I damn well needed to put down sooner rather than later.

It came at me again. I had enough sense to know the baton would be worthless against those scales. I exchanged it for my gunlight, deftly removing it from my shoulder as I shifted the setting and attempted to aim. I got a bead on the creature and fired several pulses of concentrated radiation, hoping to slow it down. I barely managed to clip a leathery wing before it was on me.

I put up an arm, giving it something to chomp on besides my neck. It seemed to like the taste of my armguard as it clamped on and wouldn't let go. The teeth wouldn't penetrate—but I felt the hot breath, it and a couple dozen tiny blades working together. The suit would only sustain so much for so long. I did my own little dance, stumbling about while trying my damnedest to stay on my feet while grabbing the vamper holstered on my left hip. The beast was clawing at my reaching hand and the hip I was reaching for. It succeeded in severing the holster; the vamper fell into the snow, half-buried under the several inches that had already fallen, soon to be fully buried under the inches more to come; and me, stumbling backward through it all while being chomped on, might end up buried with it.

My free hand didn't stop working; it managed to snag my semiautomatic. I unloaded three bullets into the creature before thinking about it. Conventional weapons were futile even at this range—even with something as powerful as a .50 caliber. The heat was getting to me. I was sweating even though the suit's temp controls were working overtime. The creature's constant pawing and clawing was screwing with the normal operations. My arm felt like a marshmallow—and I hoped to heaven that was just a psychological trick more than an actual fact.

Either way, I had to get my vamper. I'd figured this creature, whatever else it was, was primarily a creature of light. *Dirty* light, maybe—but still *light*. That's what allowed it to shift. That's what gave it its power. And my vamper would damn sure suck it away.

We tussled some more through the forest, beyond the range of the pink snowstorm. The creature's clawing felt less and less like a massage. I tried banging myself—creature-first—against a tree. No luck. I only ended up knocking myself to the ground. The creature stayed on me. And some of the armadillo-rats, who'd fled the snow, ambled near me. I reflexively grabbed one of the little bastards and shoved the thing in the dragon-goat's face. Agitated, the rat bastard released its fumes. No doubt of like origin, the damned thing had an effect on the other creature. The dragon-goat loosened its jaw grip just enough for me to whack it away. Feeling equal parts pissed and frisky, I grabbed another armadillo-rat and had it ready when the thing lunged at me again, its mouth agape for another chomp. I shoved the armadillo-rat in the dragon-goat's mouth; it immediately and predictably released its noxious fumes. The dragon-goat's hot breath no doubt only made matters worse for both of them.

Now free and with some time purchased, I scrambled back into the storm and in the general direction of the dropped vamper. Wherever it was, it had now been fully buried by the snow. I gripped my gunlight, adjusted its settings, and shot a steady beam, scanning the area where I thought I'd last seen the vamper while melting a good amount of the pink crystals with radiation until I saw a hint of it. I hunched over and snatched it just as the little dragon-goat got back on my ass—or, more accurately, on my backpack. Most of its claws dug in and got a good grip, while a loose foreclaw scratched and swiped at my helmet, possibly trying to loosen it, pry it off, or maybe even crack it open.

I attempted to run but only ended up trudging toward the nearest tree, ignoring the pain at the back of my neck—in the space the creature found between the helmet and my suit—as I loosened the pack's front straps. I picked up speed as I neared the tree and ran past it, quickly turning my body midway as I fully snapped the straps, slamming both the pack and the creature—with its too-deep grip—into the tree. Both pack and creature fell to the ground, along with some of the snow loosened from branches. I pivoted, aimed my vamper, and fired.

Both darts hit the dragon-goat: one in its chest, the other in its head. Scales or no scales, the vamper's darts were designed to penetrate even the most obstinate surfaces, and I wasted no time draining as much as energy as I could from the bastard as I hurriedly affixed the gunlight to the vamper, giving the drained energy someplace to go. The gunlight redirected the energy when I, a little off-balance, sloppily aimed and fired the device in the dragon-goat's direction. The intent was to hit it with a sustained beam, knocking it out for the count. But I missed and only ended up illuminating its escape route. When I released the trigger and began to try again, the wounded creature quickly shifted back to goat form. The darts fell free from its body as the creature gamely trotted away from me.

I checked myself for serious injuries and then gathered all my stuff. I reattached my backpack in a hurry and hustled after the creature the best I could. It left purplish tracks in the snow. Beyond, out of the storm patch, its tracks were a luminous green that faded quickly. I kept after it, though, not necessarily intending to finish it off, but more out of a hope it would lead me to one or more of its masters. I followed it for a bit till I saw some other tracks, just as small but more human. The girl. She'd fled the scene once the dragon-goat had attacked me, but her tracks were still relatively fresh.

The dragon-goat had a little pep in its steps, had regained some of its energy, but it was out of fight. It now ran through the forest like quicksilver. I, like slower gold, kept on the girl's trail. Until it stopped. I adjusted my visor's setting. I still saw nothing, but my hunter's intuition told me there was something on the ground I just couldn't see. My helmet's audial sensors picked up a hint of it. I adjusted them and caught the song. It determined which direction to go—so I went.

I was being led. I knew it, but I couldn't help it for shit. I followed a winding and untrodden path for what seemed like several years until I entered a clearing, giving me a direct full view to the front of a nicer structure than I was expecting: a cozy, two-story cabin on flat land. I'd no doubt there was a hidden story underneath, both literally and metaphorically.

In the cleared space halfway between the trees and the structure was Raker. Straight as a tent pole, he stood facing the structure. He'd a Smith & Wesson .500 in his right hand, firmly gripped but not necessarily at the ready; it was pointed toward the ground, not of much use—though the super-stunner grenade he was gripping in the other hand may've been his planned first offense.

I began to case the place from a distance. My initial look had been a straight-on view of the front, where a gable roof overlapped a wide balcony on the upper floor. It appeared the second-story balcony doors were mostly glass but as black as pitch. The balcony would've been a good position for an inhabitant to take a stand and pick off invaders as they emerged from the trees—assuming they emerged from the front as I did. But it was empty at the moment. Even the windows on the lower level were dark. There was a wraparound porch, which in one sense seemed to welcome comers from all sides. Several dozen feet of cleared land also surrounded the cabin. As I completed my wide walk-around, I saw that from either level the structure would have no views of anything, not even a lake or stream. Seclusion was the cabin's primary purpose.

Safe cabins were owned and operated by deviant-hunters and were intended to be used temporarily by other hunters when they were far from home, on a hunt, and needed a safe place to stay and stock up on supplies. Every few months or so, a hunter in charge of maintaining a particular cabin was supposed to come out and make sure the place was not only still standing but also sufficiently stocked with food and gear. This one had somehow fallen off the radar a while ago.

I stopped my walk where I'd begun it, at the front, behind Raker. He hadn't moved. There was no need to bother with stealth or camouflage at this point. But I also didn't see the need to stand as still as an ice cube.

Neither did the cabin. The structure seemed to be trembling as I approached it. The closer I got, the more it shook. Maybe that's what had stopped Raker in his tracks. The cabin seemed like it might collapse at any moment—or shape-shift. Raker had a good view of the show to come. I was two steps behind him now.

"You believe this shit?" Without turning, he spoke in a near-whisper, maybe to me, maybe to himself.

"Have no choice but to." I passed him and kept on toward the cabin. Raker caught up, walked by my side, both of us no doubt on unconscious alert to anything that might try to spring out at us. As we got closer, I discovered no surprises. The wood continued to undulate, pulsing with movement. Raker stopped again, just beyond the porch. I got in closer, within a foot of the wood, as I shifted the setting on my visor to magnification.

At first, the wood seemed to be just a dense collection of trembling grains of darkly hued rice. On closer inspection, it was like the wood was overwhelmingly infested with termites. Not any termites that could exist in our own world, but something *like* termites that had come from another realm and drew energy from a strong psychic and electro-magnetic power. The bugs weren't eating the wood; they were modifying it. As they consumed the cabin, they partially digested and regurgitated it, turning the wood from our world into a product that was mostly of theirs. I didn't see *all* of this, of course. But I remembered the science portion of my training in dealing with deviants and their tricks.

I tried to look through one of the side windows, adjusting my visor through a range of settings. The windows may as well have been slabs of onyx—very likely something from another realm. No way was I peering through them.

"I'm going in." I sauntered toward the front door.

"Frank..."

I ignored Raker, who still hadn't set foot on the porch, as

I focused on the door itself. It was no different from the infested walls. My visor didn't have any suitable X-ray setting, yet deviants could see through many objects with ease. Was Graham staring at me right now?

"*Frank.*" Raker put a little extra bass in his voice. "If you're going to do this, you think the fuckin' front door is the smartest way?"

"For me, yeah. You think they don't already know we're here?" I readied my revolver. My arm was sore (goddamned goat), but it didn't affect my grip. "You circle round; there's another balcony at the back. And a back door. Find another way in . . . or wait for me out here. Your choice." I'd weighed the options and made my choice. This may well end up being a blackball hunt. I accepted that. Still facing the door, I removed two blackballs from the pouch on my belt and slipped them inside the snug little pockets at the base of my gloves.

I grasped the knob. With my gloves on, I wasn't really worried about feeling anything on my fingers, but the vibration that ran across my palm and up my arm made me think briefly that my exoskeletal uniform had been damaged by the creature in the forest. Even if so, I couldn't dwell on it, just deal with it.

The door was unlocked. As I opened it, the interior lights flickered on—all of them, it seemed. I was tense and ready, but nothing made a noise or came at me. Only the foul, dank air made a feeble assault. It was like rotting eggs: potent enough to bypass my helmet's filters but otherwise having no real effect. Nothing else came my way. Nothing but the faint hum of electricity. Nice perk for such a remote cabin. But I knew it wasn't a local gas and electric company powering this haven.

My otherworld-termite theory—based on learning and

in-the-field experience—was further bolstered by what I saw the moment I almost tripped over the threshold. The rules of physics were slightly off in here, so my suit's balance negotiators were a bit tipsy as well. And it was no small wonder that the floor plan in no way fit what I'd seen on the outside. The living room that I'd entered, which by no means was the entirety of the first floor, had at least twice the circumference one would judge by viewing the cabin from outside. Instead of letting that fact or the funny physics throw me, I did what I could to get an inventory of any potential hostiles and of anything that might be danger-ously out of place. I mostly saw the knickknacks one would expect in a log cabin home. A few slat-back wooden chairs, all of them pushed to the walls, made way for the nicer furniture.

This had been a real cabin at some point, but after the family moved in, something else took over. The question was, who had more sway—the deviants or the something else? The White Fire Virus was more than a disease that conferred otherworldly abilities; it was also a key to opening the door to another realm, an evil realm. This place was built in part from materials from that other dimension, the realm where the deviants got their secret wisdom and esoteric knowledge. I'd no doubt that any lost soul who stumbled upon this place was disposed of, one way or another.

I kept a firm grip on my .44 Mag and kept my left hand loose, ready to grab anything else I might need from my belt or vest as I steadily made my way over the uneven floor. Up ahead on the left was a darkened opening that perhaps led to a dining room.

The dark mocha leather couches and recliners may as well have been small, hibernating bulls or some other mammals. They appeared to inflate and deflate as if they were breathing in this musty air. The tables and lamps and random knickknacks were all crystal and glass. My eyes were so focused on the furniture, anticipating its arousal and inevitable assault, that I almost didn't see the most obvious creature in the center of the room, on the rug. The *goat*. My grip tightened on the .44 Mag while my free hand reached for the vamper.

The tingle came back—stronger, more intense, and this time in both arms. My hands seized up as the sensation spread throughout my body. I dropped the revolver. I couldn't get to the vamper. I couldn't even kick at the damned goat as it ambled over, grabbed the gun with its mouth, and scampered from the room.

I had a faint suspicion the musty air in the room had something to do with my condition, but the thought remained unfinished as two arms encircled me from behind, trapping my arms at my side. As strong as two-by-four planks of wood but as pliable as wet noodles, they coiled like springs, squeezed me like an accordion, and stripped me of my vest and backpack before letting go. I still couldn't move my arms. They were bound to my side with some kind of rope. Something—again from behind—grabbed the sides of my helmet, jerked, yanked, twisted, and then jerked again. I tried to shrug, turn, twist away, but before I could tell which way was which, my helmet was lifted off my head and tossed across the room. It landed with a *crack* near the door. I had nothing to say about it. I had other words as I found my aggressor standing less than three feet in front of me. Only my prescription glasses provided a barrier between my eyes and the deranged visage of Marcus Graham.

French cropped hair and a short-boxed beard framed

the familiar rectangular face. The copper streaks in his hair competed with the gray—but the color that drew my attention was the blazing orange of Graham's eyes. I shifted my gaze downward and saw he was decked out in a hunter's uniform. One very similar to mine, sans the vest or backpack.

Feeling was coming back to me, to my legs at least. Maybe my paralysis had more to do with Graham's machinations than the nasty air, for it seemed that now that he had me where he wanted me, he could ease up on his concentration and do other things. Like taunt me.

I wasn't looking at his face, but I heard him open his mouth, the first guttural noise from his throat indicating he was about to say something. I lowered my shoulder and launched myself in his direction. He didn't step aside. Graham simply kept his hips under him as he hunched, grabbed me, and flipped me over the couch and onto a throw rug that may as well have been flypaper. I couldn't move as he scrambled over, took my semiautomatic from my thigh holster, and pointed it at me.

"Know what I used to do to home invaders back in the day, buddy?" He pointed the gun at my forehead and made small circular motions. "Particularly those that threaten my family?" The gun still had several rounds left. At this range there was no surviving. The look in his eye told me he was ready to canoe me. I listened hard for Raker, anyone, but heard nothing, not a sound other than the electricity and Graham's breathing. He smiled. "Lucky you. I'm a different man now." He tucked the gun into his thigh holster.

I wanted to threaten the SOB. Better yet, I wanted to get at him. But all I could do was stall while trying to get free. Failing that, I'd try to set off one of the blackballs—taking us both out, finalizing the hunt.

Graham dragged a wooden slat-back chair away from its corner, set it backward at my feet, and sat, facing me, his arms crossed over the high back. "You know, I knew they'd eventually send *you*."

I fixed my eyes on him as best as I could. "How did it happen, Marc?"

His face contorted. His smile was that of a clown swallowing candy-covered thumbtacks. "Don't you know?" He spoke with a constricted throat as if he really were swallowing something that was cutting and drawing blood as he slowly choked it down. "Didn't your masters tell you? Didn't they even give you a hint?"

"I want to hear it from your own lips."

He shrugged, stood, and removed the gun from the holster. He then paced around the rug, clockwise and counter, tossing the gun from hand to hand and sporadically launching into hysterical laughter. Eventually, the gun settled in one hand; with the other, he ran his spazzy fingers through his hair, attempting to rake what was already a mess into total chaos. He was a madman, disturbed further by no sleep. I'd come to that edge a few times myself; unlike Graham, I'd never tipped over. Presently, though, I maintained a balance of trying to struggle free and trying to get my fingers on a blackball, nudging it from its pouch into my glove.

"Went through a bad patch early on in the marriage," Graham muttered, still pacing after completing a circuit around the rug maybe half a dozen times. "Crept out a lot on Linda. She was doing the same. Still don't know which one of us contracted it first. Which or whatever, both of us, we *snatched* the Virus. The White Fire Virus."

I tried to sit up again. No go. "And the kids?"

"Born with it."

"Not what I heard."

He stopped pacing and looked at me, shaking his head. "Damn it, Frank, what do you—" He paused and tried to calm himself. "Linda and I were doing all this before the kids were born. We both had it and didn't know it before we tried to conceive."

"If that were true," I said, "the kids would've been quarantined. You and Linda too."

"It was latent, Frank. None of us manifested symptoms until much later."

"They run tests on all children born these days." I hardened my gaze. "Children born in hospitals, that is."

He circled back to what he started to say earlier. "What do you think, Frank?"

"That you or your deranged wife gave it to your young kids," I said. "On purpose. After they were born."

He kept his eyes on me as he held the semiautomatic in his left hand and tightened his grip. A malformed smile marred his face as he lowered his head. He rubbed his chin with the fingers of his right hand as he pointed the gun in my general direction before slowly pointing the muzzle toward the top of his own head. He paused, then used the gun to scratch his scalp. "One of the best at what he does . . ." Like the sound of an approaching train on rickety tracks, the manic, abbreviated laugh built until it seemed to come out full force. Graham brandished the gun in my general direction. "Could teach a master class . . . ." He darted the barrel at me like a sewing needle as he leaned down closer. "And still too *fuckin'* stupid to know an outright *fuckin'* dirty lie when he hears one."

I tried to ignore the barrel that was now aimed squarely at my forehead, just as I tried to ignore Graham's *mind screw*. Terrorists and criminals of all stripes attempted it, but it was a bold, neon signature of The Infinite Definite, and often done successfully. The result: one's thoughts were so twisted, a man became his own worst enemy, inflicting mental and physical harm on himself. Mind screwing led to body ripping. *Never listen to their lies.* But maybe the flypaper rug was listening. Maybe some of its properties fed off some of Graham's mental energies. I was making progress in my struggle to peel myself off. A blackball would work fine if I could get it through the glove and let it rest on a fingertip for a few minutes. It'd work so much better if I could snatch off a glove and pinch the ball between two fingers. Still, in the building anxiety of my own impending suicide and successful hunt, I couldn't help but wonder: *Just where the hell's Raker?*

Graham seemed unconcerned with my actions; he seemed more focused on my words. "Has it ever occurred to you, Frank, that someone might be lying to you?"

"Yeah. It's occurred to me that you are."

He grinned shakily. "Untrusting . . . A *useful* skill. But prejudice *isn't*. You're blinded by what I've become, buddy."

"Any reason I shouldn't be?"

"Let me guess who sent you. Schupbach and Watton. Am I right? Am I right? *Amiright*? And you verified nothing, *right*? Didn't reverify credentials. Didn't challenge them or run any tests. Because that's not how you operate these days. You and your damned club. Your damned hunting parties."

"Let's not get into who has been *damned* here."

"No, *let's*—*God*-bender, *Deviant*-Hunter, *Fool*-Player— whatever you think you are. Schupbach and Watton, those two and those they're linked up with, they keep sending folks after us because of what we *know*. My family—my very *good* family—has disposed of them all. That's how I got this nifty uniform." Despite the rising intensity of his voice, he eased up with the gun, waving it all around, aiming it every-where but at me as he gesticulated wildly. "We moved here and got fortified. Thought we'd be safe and left alone. But *no*, the drug mongers keep sending their blind dogs of war. Putting up false propaganda on the net. Making it easily findable by those who think they're too clever by half and know how to look."

Another exertion made me grunt. "Rant all you want." My shoulders were free. The binds around my arms had slackened. I felt I was getting there, inch by inch. "The bottom line is, it's over for you."

"No, buddy—the bottom line is that you've been taken in, and this is a home invasion. My family and I have a right to defend what's ours. But hell, I haven't forgotten my manners. You are a guest in my home. What kind of host would I be if I didn't ask you to break bread with me?" His grin took on more twisted dimensions. "We can discuss our differences over a nice, hearty meal. Doesn't that sound nice? Doesn't that sound special? What do you think?"

I thought what was coming next might make me vomit.

He tossed the gun onto the couch, then reached down with both hands and throttled me, choking me, while he pulled me up off the rug. A *para-taze*—my name for his bare fingers at my unprotected neck paralyzing me just enough to prevent any sudden offensive maneuvers while jolting enough to keep me moving at his direction and discretion. We didn't go far. He forced me into the slat-back chair next to the rug. Almost as if they had a mind of their own (hell, maybe they did), the binds around my arms and midsection attached themselves to the chair, wrapping around it like agitated snakes—or so the whole motion felt.

Graham scrambled behind me, grabbed the sides of the back support, and lifted me up as if I were just a sack made of skin and filled with packing peanuts. He carried the chair and me in front of him as he walked. I struggled. The binds were like rubber hoses but stronger and more flexible. The longer I pulled against them, the more they gave. But when I gave, they snapped back, clenching even tighter. I stopped after a bit; if they clenched any tighter, I wouldn't be able to breathe.

Beyond the living area, we entered the adjacent dining room. A faint mossy green haze filled the air. Graham set me down at the head of the oblong dining table. At the other end, beyond the chair, was the kitchen. No wall or door separated the rooms. My sight went directly to the tall woman with red-violet hair—*Linda,* I presumed. She was wearing a green nightgown and standing next to a complicated machine that appeared equal parts metallic, porcelain, and *organic.*

The woman met my eyes, smiled, and exited the kitchen to the left. I focused fully on the device. Its base—or the part that rested on the floor—was situated like an oven, but with its circular door, it looked more like a high efficiency washer or dryer. A row of cabinets provided a buffer between it and the refrigerator on one side and a door leading outside on the other. Four silver tubes were attached to the top as if rising up from the eyes on the stove. They weren't pure silver; they were silvery pink like the skin of minnows. The ringed tubes extended up, curving to run perpendicular to the ceiling and ending in a large gray box that hung directly over the table. Like the furniture in the other room, the overhead box seemed to be breathing. There was no chandelier, no ceiling lights. On the underside of the breathing box were random spots of various sizes and colors, all glowing and providing more than enough illumination (in various hues) for the dining area. I had a large platter in front of me. At three other areas on the table—

at three o'clock, nine-o'clock, and twelve o'clock—were large, transparent salad bowls. I liked the looks of none of it.

Linda reentered the kitchen and my view, leading Juliano, who'd been stripped naked, bound, and gagged, to the other end of the dining-room table. He seemed drugged and didn't put up much of a struggle. Not that it would probably do much good. His arms hung straight down at his sides. His binds, which looked like eels, wrapped around his chest and waist, keeping his arms tight, like mine. Did the binds act like eels, providing mild electric shocks to keep him in line? I wouldn't know; my binds didn't touch my skin. And Juliano was in no position to talk about it. The gag hanging halfway out of his mouth was someone's underwear, wet with blood.

Graham chuckled. "Yeah, she had some fun with him first. Quick and dirty. But I got a little tired of his screams of passion—know what I mean? And wouldn't you know? The tongue *jumped* right out, like it was happy to go!"

I'd tried to keep my composure, but now I couldn't hold it back; the dam burst, and I let loose a torrent of curses at Graham, his dumb wife, and any other perpetrator in this damned place. Graham only laughed as he whisked out of the room and Linda positioned Juliano in a chair at the opposite end of the table.

A door opened in section of the cabin I couldn't see; I thought of Raker, *hoped* for Raker, as I heard the sounds of a scuffle but only saw Graham returning—with Krissy. He carried her above his above his head like a raised barbell. Her hands and feet were bound, and she'd been stripped down to her undergarments: violet sports bra and panties, all tattered and muddy. She must've been stuffed in a closet after being brought here.

I stopped cursing. It was a waste of energy and unprofessional. I needed to start thinking.

My first thought: How the fuck had he gotten them out of their gear so quickly? Juliano and Krissy were both trained combatants. But then so was Marc—trained in all sorts of dark ways and mannerisms. And his kids . . . This dirty son of a bitch. He and his kids had gone out into the forest to meet us, setting HotSpot traps. Space was displaced in HotSpots; and sometimes time ran differently in them. The "fifth hunter" had been Marc. He'd laid some kind of whammy on me and maybe Raker, too, giving himself and the kids enough time to jump and snatch Juliano and Krissy with relative ease.

Graham now strapped Krissy in at a seat in front of a bowl. She seemed just as drugged out of it as Juliano, but she occasionally straightened and shook a bit as if electric shocks were periodically going through her body. After binding her feet—something he hadn't done with me—he reached deeper under the table and came out with a bulging, leathery sack. Graham heaved and dropped it on the table, spilling some of its contents: stuff that had been stripped from the belts, vests, and backpacks of the other hunters. "Let's see what Santy Marc has got for the naughty-or-nice . . ." Ignoring the stuff that had spilled onto the table, he rummaged through the sack while bearing his now-familiar wild-eyed grin.

He retrieved a few items—a Glock, a super-stunner grenade, and a fist-size pouch—carefully and with great theatricality placing each of them in turn on the platter in front of me. He emptied the pouch onto the platter—it contained three blackballs—then he got in my face.

"Would you like to say grace?"

I avoided his eyes and looked at his lips, pale and wet. "The *fuck* is this, Marc?"

"I want to find out just how naughty or nice you really are, buddy. You hunters waste *us*. *My* kind. *Why*? Because of our condition? A condition we really can't help?"

"You can help it. You can turn yourself in."

"To be *wasted*."

"For *treatment*."

He guffawed. "I'm not *that* far gone. There's *no* cure. Only *prayer* in the holy place. The only treatment, if you turn me in, is a bullet in the temple. That's why they sent *you*." He glanced toward his wife, who'd made an unintelligible noise. He chuckled. "Or maybe I turn *you* in, buddy. Inside *out*. What else is a hunter to do with his prey, hmm?"

My eyes darted between him and his wife, then Juliano and Krissy. I growled, "What the hell are you talking about?"

"You, *prey*, were hunted. Schupbach and Watton were the hounds. And the hunters, well . . . Anyways, you were *caught*. Ready to be field dressed. House *undressed*." His wife made another weird, guttural noise. "Parts of you are consumable, parts are waste. Soldiers are waste. Collateral damage—who gives a damn? *Waste*."

His rambling was descending further into incoherence, far beyond sense—maybe beyond reason. I couldn't allow myself to feed into it. But I couldn't quite zone out either. I tried to think of new ways to get free.

"You infect others," I said. "Dinner parties, orgies . . ."

"Lies. We protect ourselves from hunters and other slayers—like *you*. We stay away from others. Feast only in self-defense."

"And this place? This hell house?"

"Our benefactor." His face relaxed into a satisfied smile. "Do you know what the Virus is, Frank? Do you *really* know?

It was a *creature*. The *government's* creature. A *creation* of government. A weapon to get rid of certain undesirables, certain elements in society. Useless groups who were sucking up taxpayer dollars, they could be made to give back by becoming *weapons* of the government. And the viral-free government operatives who'd seen the light, who understood the truth of what was going on? Well, hell, they could get the same benevolent and beneficent and beautiful *treatment*."

I grunted with an exertion that did me no good. "What are you saying?"

"I'm saying you need to *submit* to the new reality, buddy. *Join* us. Join our war against the perpetrators of what you call deviance. Or just die here. What do you think?"

I looked at the blackballs on the platter in front of me: the beautiful black pellets. They were essentially suicide pills, set off by one's fingerprints and intended to take out a high-end target at close range. They worked by exciting the electrical activity in the nervous system, amping it up beyond capacity, and shooting out a potent web of psychic electricity—or at least that's how I understood it. Obviously, I'd never used one before; as I considered the implications now, the psycho couple seemed to take my silence as rejection of their offer.

"Maybe you need some encouragement," Graham continued. "Something like a rah-rah speech, hmm?" He positioned himself behind me. Linda positioned herself behind Juliano. She clasped her left hand on the back of his neck and lifted, pulling Juliano to his feet. Placing her right hand at the small of his back, she guided him back into the kitchen and toward the oversize oven or washer or whatever the hell it was.

It was neither.

At their approach, the contraption's door twisted open counterclockwise, on its own, until it was a gaping black hole with serrated edges. *A mouth.* Linda kicked at the back of Juliano's legs, apparently trying to bring him to his knees. It didn't work. He was fighting it, resisting her. She thrashed him across the head a few times, further weakening him, then tried again. Juliano crumpled to his knees; Linda shoved his head toward the gaping maw. A faint, fuchsia glow appeared from somewhere deep in the black space, pulsing like a radiant, salivating tongue.

"You led them into this," Graham said. "*You're* the head of this party. *They* suffer."

My binds loosened. Graham was loosening them with his mind. Or maybe it was the creature, the one whose mouth stood open, ready to accept a sacrifice. Whoever was doing it had freed me enough that I could grab an item on the platter.

Graham remained behind me. He made no move. But he seemed to know what I was thinking.

"Take your shot, buddy. Be naughty or nice."

That's when I got it. *Straight from his damned playbook.* I could spare Juliano by killing him, but that wouldn't spare my soul—or so Graham believed. Give someone a damned-near-impossible choice . . .

But Graham didn't know me as well as he thought. Here, my choice seemed clear—go for the Glock and take out Linda. Did she or Graham really think I couldn't get off a good shot at this range? I slid my arms out of the ties and placed my hands on the table. As if reading my mind, Linda enshrouded herself in folding waves of red-violet flames. It was just an illusion, an effect of light. If I had my helmet or my specs, I could easily see through it to the deviant woman underneath—no dice with just glasses. Only Juliano remained clear as day. I could easily plug him but not her. The Glock was out of the question. The super-stunner was an even worse choice. The devices were similar to regular stun grenades but much stronger. They also had two settings: Starburst and Thundershower. The first released a burst of light so intense it would blind a human and do much worse to a deviant (instilling images that would brutally assault the senses into submission), but only if the deviant was not expecting it. The second setting released a burst of intense static that effectively delivered several rapid punches to the brain and sharp pinches to the nervous system in a matter of seconds.

The latter setting would kill Juliano anyway—and probably Krissy, too, at this range—leaving Graham behind me to finish me off. The other setting would be even more disastrous. Graham knew what the devices did; maybe Linda did too. For them, the Starburst explosion would be a *gift*, a bounty of light one or both could easily contain and manipulate into an electromagnetic assault against us. And the blackballs, I'd assumed, were just a joke—three suicide pills. One for each hunter in the room. *Where in the hell was Raker?*

Graham let out a sigh as if he'd been holding his breath. "You've got a time limit, buddy: sixty more seconds of sand."

Yeah, this was his sick idea of a puzzle: one where all answers are really wrong, but just one is justifiable. A lesser hunter might've turned in on himself, turned *on* himself, betrayed himself. A lesser hunter was one without my oath. But I had an answer—justifiable and right. Graham was the ultimate target. Everyone else was expendable, including me.

I stood suddenly, thrusting my chair back to create more distance between Graham and me. Then I snatched the

Glock and grenade and spun around, getting off two rounds. I only winged Graham in the shoulder before he clocked me with a left hook, sending a numbness throughout half my body and forcing me to drop the gun. I made damn sure not to drop the grenade.

He lunged. The numbness left, and—ready this time—I grabbed him with my free hand. Using the strength of my hips and my shoulders—and his own weight against him—I positioned him between me and the table. I held him in place with my forearm under his neck. I had seconds. I prepared to flip the switch on the device, setting it to Thundershower, before tossing it toward the kitchen. I'd snap Graham's neck immediately upon release.

He thrashed about and bit at my arm, sending the platter to the floor and shattering it, scattering the blackballs. I glanced toward the kitchen and saw a wall of light. I couldn't tell if Juliano was safe or not. I switched tactics. I needed to take out the immediate and biggest threat now.

As Graham continued to struggle fiercely, I gave him some room and maneuvered to get behind him. Then I tossed the inactive grenade a couple of feet from me on the table and embraced him, connecting and tightening my hands under his sternum. The grenade was still within arm's reach.

For all his talk of dressing and undressing, he'd neglected to strip me of my uniform. A mistake. A bigger mistake was that he remained in his pilfered one. As he struggled to get free, even resorting to turning invisible and releasing a fusillade of radio static my way, I fiddled with a switch on my wristband, reversing my suit's temp-control. The effects weren't extreme—it would've had no effect on the dragon creature that had its jaws on me. But for a quick-and-dirty shock to the system of something that was once a man . . . of something wearing a uniform he most likely didn't know how to use? *Yep.* The surface of my suit fluctuated between the extremes of temperature—rapidly—causing Graham's suit to automatically react. The fluctuations made him unbend the light around him, turning him visible while he tried to control his own body temperature inside a suit he couldn't control. Now that he was too preoccupied with his own comfort to attack, I wrapped my arms around his unprotected head and squeezed. My suit clung to his skin, sending him an electrostatic shock. The attack lasted less than ten seconds, which was enough time for Graham to feel all of it but not enough time for him to protect himself from any of it. He reacted in my favor by jerking and then going limp as he slumped toward the table.

I used all my weight to pin him down, throttling him with one hand as I reached for the grenade. I got it, and when I released his throat, he opened his mouth, desperate to take in air. This made it easier for me to get a good grip on his lower jaw, forcing it down as I wedged the grenade halfway in and flipped the switch for Starburst. Whether he was expecting a generous burst of light or not, an explosive device in the mouth was still an explosive device in the mouth.

I felt a sizzling shock at the back of my knees and reflexively fell backward, releasing my grip on Graham. Looking to my left, I caught a glimpse of the girl, still in her pajamas, and—presumably—her brother, also in dingy PJs, standing nearby in the opening between the dining and living rooms. The boy nimbly caught the freed live grenade Graham tossed at him and in turn tossed it into the living room, possibly toward the front door. It may've made it outside, or it may've gone off in midair; either way, the result was like a sustained flash of green lightning. The kids—their eyes aglow—seemed to be soaking it up. This was going to be a problem. My eyes darted for the Glock I'd dropped. As I was closest to the floor, I hoped to get to it before anyone else.

Then the boy screamed.

I recognized the *zzztt* sound that prompted it, and I recognized the kids' attacker even before I looked up. As Raker had gotten the drop on me in the warehouse, he'd done the same here with the boy. From somewhere in the living room Raker had gotten close enough to sting the boy with a vamper and feed the drained energy into his gunlight, which he fired immediately at the girl. Her screams joined her brother's.

I sensed movement above me and to my right. Graham was lunging. I tuck-and-rolled clear while trying to get to my feet and shouting at Raker, "*Krissy! Juliano!*"

With all the chaos of shouting, screaming, crying—added to another infernal *hiss* that rose up from nowhere, filling the room with steam—Raker no doubt didn't hear me, or else he was too preoccupied with the kids. I said little more, being preoccupied with Graham, who was on me the moment I was back on two feet.

We slugged and wrestled, with me mostly defending myself, before he got me in a hug and tried the same trick I'd earlier used on him. With his supernatural abilities amplifying the effect, he had an edge. Light exploded in my eyes as burning ice shot through my bones. I saw nothing but electric blue blanketed with sheets of diaphanous frost.

By the time my vision was somewhat clear, I was in a full nelson, forced to face Krissy. Raker and the kids were gone, as was Juliano. The wife stood by the oven, unshrouded and bearing an unsettling grin. She was foaming at the mouth. So was the oven. Its mouth had closed, but it was dripping a thick, red liquid.

I wanted to vomit. I knew immediately what had happened. Though the oven-like contraption sounded more like a washing machine as it churned and burned, it was neither. The stove was the mouth of this beast of a cabin; the creature was not only the structure but much of the furniture and other decorations as well. It had come here from another realm, consumed the cabin, and became, in part, much of what it had consumed. As a result, it had turned inside out, folded in on itself. Graham and his family were its caretakers and its disciples. Ownership went both ways. The silver tubes that sprang out like arches from the machine hit the ceiling and slithered along its grainy, speckled surface. They were like intestines. The tubes that now descended from the box like elongated metallic-blue elephant trunks—glistening, writhing—were like something I wasn't even sure I could name. The trunks fixed their positions to point over the three salad bowls and, section by section, expanded, becoming engorged as they aimed. I guessed what was coming even before they shit out Juliano's partially digested body parts into the wide, deep bowls, including the one in front of Krissy. The slushy, overflowing mess contained bits and fluids, human-body materials already digested once and divorced from their adhesive soul, which had no doubt already evaporated into another realm. But there were foreign substances in there as well. As I tried to hold it together while gazing at this blasphemous swill, I saw grayish tubular creatures the size of thumbs and white pellets the size of fingernails that were swimming and crawling about the disgorged matter, having their own feast.

"Blood and brain and body bits . . ." Graham intoned. "Over maggots, worms, and beetles. Talk about a soup for the soul, heh?"

I cursed him and struggled more fiercely as Linda, glistening, not all of it from sweat, sauntered over. She put her slimy hand at the back of Krissy's neck. The hunter had a sickly pallor to her. Krissy was more than drugged; she seemed half-dead already. But like Juliano before, she tried to resist; she tried to fight. I could see the hairs on Linda's arm raising; I could hear (or maybe I imagined) the electro-magnetic static traveling from the deviant's fingers to the nerves in Krissy's neck. Her head nodded downward; Linda put her free hand on the back of Krissy's head and pushed her face toward the overflowing bowl. She didn't release her hold as Krissy opened her mouth and lapped it up.

"Like a dog, eh, buddy?" Graham cackled in my ear. "Like a running dog of the government. *They're* responsible for all of this."

I struggled even more, this time shaking the table enough so that the bag spilled all of its contents. Maybe that hadn't all been me; the entire house seemed to be trembling as if it were experiencing post-digestive effects.

Graham loosened his hold just a little; he didn't let me free, but he gave me just enough leeway to get free if I really wanted. "Let her eat. She's with the enemy. *Our* enemy. How do you think she knew where to find us? How did she get info on me so quickly?"

Mind screwing with me. He had to be. I struggled more fiercely as I saw Krissy's skin changing. Hell, her whole body composition seemed to change as parts of her grayed and other body parts lightened. Finally, she stopped moving altogether. Her body slumped over the bowl as if it had devolved into clay, half of it already hardened. Maybe it was just an illusion, but there was no mistaking that she was dead.

"She's going in next," Graham said. "Then *you'll* get to eat up." Linda cackled. "You're the only one being given a choice," Graham continued. "Free will and all that, hmm? Let's see if you still got it—*hunter*."

I took a quick survey of the objects on the table within reach, the ones that had earlier spilled from the sack. Many of them were now covered or rendered useless by the slop. A few choice items weren't: a spice canister, a Glock, and a few Skrapnel capsules. Graham tried to force me down into a chair; I gave up on my struggle just a little to let him think he could do it, but when he changed his body position and released a little pressure, I slipped out of his grip and lunged for the table.

Slightly quicker on the uptake than her husband, Linda rushed toward me, but the spice canister was in my hand, and—as she was no more than three feet away from me—I was able to spice her good. The stuff worked a lot like pepper spray but was specifically designed to damage the parasites in a deviant's eyes. Linda closed her eyes, but I'd gotten enough spray on her face to ensure her senses would be in disarray for a bit when she opened them again. I didn't stay put to see the results as I heard Graham yowling, closing in.

I grabbed a handful of Skrapnel capsules as I twisted out of his way. I gave myself a little extra distance, taking a few quick steps into the living room before I tossed the capsules at Graham's face with as much force as I could muster. The capsules were filled with tiny metallike jacks; when the capsules burst—ideally upon impact against a deviant's bare skin—the Skrapnel was absorbed into the skin, making it painfully difficult for a deviant to use their light-manipulation abilities, particularly anything that involved casting illusions or turning invisible. Three of the capsules were a direct hit; they slowed Graham down by a fraction of a second, which was long enough for me to grab the nearest slat-back chair and break it across his shoulder and head when he resumed his rush toward me. I quickly headed to the table, avoiding Graham's body as he fell and ignoring his anguished scream as the embedded Skrapnel prevented him from sending some kind of light assault my way. I had less luck with the shrieking Linda.

Even with a face coated with spice, she was still quick on the uptake, knowing what I was going for—but she wasn't quick enough to get to the Glock before me. I spun away from her frantic grabbing, moving myself closer toward the kitchen, and in my own frantic excitement (and not a little bit of anger about what she'd done to Juliano and Krissy), I unloaded the entire magazine into her—two in the head, one in the neck. It only had three rounds. I had nothing left for Graham.

I turned his way. He'd managed to make it to the table, but the Skrapnel must've taken a bigger toll on him than I thought. The more a deviant tried to use their abilities, the more the Skrapnel dug in. Graham looked as if he'd barely survived a landmine—intact but done in. He'd reached the table's edge and had pulled himself on top, probably trying to reach a weapon. But there'd been nothing he could get his hands on, and he'd seemed to have given up, laughing and writhing on the tabletop among the slop and ruined accessories.

Guttural, grainy noises that seemed to be the audial equivalent of marrow—and undoubtedly came from some-place just as deep—made the cabin tremble ever more violently with each passing second. The damned thing was angry. Its machinelike mouth opened and closed as if it were trying again and again to scream. My thoughts raced toward my next move and settled on a narrowing lane as I moved closer to Graham.

There wasn't time to search for another gun or something that could more permanently end him. As he'd said, the hourglass was running out. Instead, I grabbed a dangling rope of the eely stuff hanging from my chair, the sticky stuff that had bound me. Whatever it was, it was partially organic, like much of the stuff in this damned cabin. It was the beast's flesh. The electrical current that seemed to run through it might excite the blackballs, but it might not. I didn't have time to think it all through. At this point I was going by intuition, not rational thought. I used the eely rope to bind three grenades—two set on Starburst, one on Thundershower—and however many blackballs I could funnel from my pouch and stick into the rope. Then I hustled back toward the kitchen and, at the right moment, tossed it into the gaping maw and dashed for the kitchen door.

My hand was on the knob, but it wouldn't move. I felt the now-familiar tingle. I was becoming incapacitated again ... *Graham.* He shouted something at me, words and noises I could hear but not even halfway decipher. It didn't matter anyway if I couldn't get out. I thought of a prayer and began to recite it aloud.

My words and Graham's exclamations were suddenly overwhelmed by an inhuman groan coming from the cabin's mouth. Maybe it was sensing oncoming indigestion. Maybe it wanted to be rid of everything that was not truly a part of it. That was my best guess as the tingle went away. I threw open the door and ran as fast as my weary muscles, suit, and adrenaline would allow me.

By the sound of it, the chain reaction was gradual—but I didn't slow up or turn around. I kept running, kept on trudging, until I was forced to the ground. Even then I tucked my head, jammed my hands against my ears, kept my eyes away.

Looking at the damned thing might do more damage than looking directly at a solar eclipse. I could guess on the effect. The creature would feast on itself in the most gluttonous manner.

All I feasted on now was dirt. I wasn't worried so much about my body; my suit, as damaged as it was, would protect me well enough. It was just my head. It had been screwed with enough for one day.

I didn't know how long I lay there. All I knew was that my hands weren't good earplugs. They were still pasted to my head when I heard someone approaching.

"You all right, man?"

Raker.

I uncovered my ears and craned my neck upward. He was still suited up, helmet and all. "Don't know." I got to my knees. "Graham?"

He shook his head. "I was on the other side of the cabin, just coming out of the forest. Watched the whole damn thing." He pulled off his helmet. "Didn't see anyone get out on my side. He could've followed you out."

He could have.

Raker was gazing toward the cabin, or what was left. I turned as well and got a good look at what appeared to be a large, uneven mound of bruised flesh in shades of dull beige and eggplant. It was riddled with glowing, smoldering chunks of crimson, jade, and colors that were indescribable, random bits and pieces that could well have been the remains of stuff the cabin had never subsumed and made part of its body. That was just a guess—and it didn't matter now. I heard a low, distant drone as I watched the pulsing mound expanding and contracting like a dying lung. Its essence was fading—to oblivion, I hoped.

I suddenly felt like I had soap in my eyes. I shut them and asked, "The kids?" It came out just above a whisper.

"Lost them in the woods." Raker spoke almost as low. "Didn't want to pursue them without you. Without ensuring Marcus Graham was—"

"Dead." I heaved myself to my feet. "I'm sure of it." Gazing at the ashes, I wasn't.

Raker grunted. "I sent out the signal for cleanup. This deep in though ..."

"Yeah." I turned my eyes up toward the sky. It had lightened to a cool gray. "We need to get back to civilization to make sure they heard it."

"You want to poke around the ashes some first?"

I almost laughed as I continued to gaze upward. We'd soon see the rosy hints of the rising sun. The gray would be washed away by fire. I compared it to the hell that had just happened down here.

"Frank?"

I lowered my eyes and shook my head as I rubbed my arms. The adrenaline had faded; I was feeling the creeping pain from tonight's sustained injuries. "I've wallowed in the dirt enough for one morning."

5

———

Raker made contacts with his HSA connections and guided them toward the site while I remained by The Machine, checking up on Frankie. She'd been having such a blast with her friend she hadn't been missing me at all. Thank God. I wasn't about to head home just yet.

Raker and I parted ways, intending to meet up again around noon at a special little place he kept in in the woods on a hill several miles away. It was not a safe cabin—the opposite, actually. In the meantime, I'd had some brief communications with Schupbach and Watton, just enough to let them know the mission was a success and to hear them tell me they'd ensure their usual damage control procedures would be put into motion. We'd have a face-to-face debrief in a few days. I gazed toward the sun as I listened to their voices, which I could practically smell from all the shit they were talking.

When we met, Raker caught me up quickly. Heartland Security's cleanup found the bodies of husband and wife among the remains of the once-living cabin, remains their scientist friends would no doubt be salivating to study. The kids had gotten away. The goat—who the fuck knew? I listened to the rundown, mechanically filtering it for key bits of info where I might need to do some cleanup on my own. Mostly, though, I focused on Graham, remembering his words, the coherent ones, the ones focusing on family. And on Schupbach and Watton.

Raker opened my eyes like the sun never could. Krissy had been one hell of a researcher, but he was no slouch. When I'd initially sent out the alert, he didn't do much digging on Graham; he'd done it on Shupbach and Watton, confirming the rumors he'd been hearing for weeks prior. He now shared that info with me.

The pair were dirtier than worms. And just as spineless. And just as blind—though I guessed I'd have to include myself in that bit of the description. After telling him what went down in the cabin from my perspective, I sipped coffee and listened to his end of it. He'd entered the cabin from the balcony at the back and into the master bedroom; while keeping an eye out for hostiles, he rooted around and gathered some interesting information. Apparently, only two of the three bedrooms had been used for sleeping. The third was used for research and gathering info, which presumably the couple had intended to disseminate one day. Raker had copped a thumb drive or two.

"Graham wasn't just blowing smoke when he said the Virus was created as a government plot," Raker said, "at least not according to the sources I've seen, which are pretty damn reliable. And that bit about him and his wife stepping out on each other? It seems both of them were targeted by Typhoid Mary types. They were infected on purpose."

I set my cup on the coffee table. "What the hell for?"

"Life, my man, is a game to some, an experience to

others, and to quite a few others, an experiment. They're always pushing the boundaries."

"But I mean, why Marc? What about him was so undesirable?" I knew the answer even as I asked the question. Still, Raker narrated my thoughts.

"He was too smart. Too *deep*. He knew about the government's plan and wanted no part of it; he truly wanted to retire and live a normal life. And apparently, they let him go. But they were secretly monitoring him, waiting for a chance to get back at him, to use him for a test case. He wasn't the only one."

I clenched my fists, wanting to punch glass or metal or something else inanimate that would make me feel it, *regret* it. I was regretting what happened to Marc: a middle-aged American man who loved his family and his country, knew its history, knew its ideals, and knew *how* to deal in order to keep the ship on course. But he knew far too much—far more than me, obviously—about how the dark network really got things done in this country and about those on the ground, deep under grassroots, where they tend to the soil the sun will never see. He was a liability. He was simply an accountant's term. Accountants didn't like accounts that didn't reconcile. And Shupbach and Watton were so far off the books, no auditor would ever even blink.

Raker passed me a disk he'd made with more details on what he'd discovered, then he made himself scarce. I made myself comfortable in The Machine as I flipped on the laptop, skimmed my oath, and put the disk in. Things made more sense, and less.

Schupbach and Watton—secret lovers. Rogue operatives themselves, they'd been injecting rogue agents with the disease for some time now, for business and for fun. They'd committed violations. Destroyed families. Frayed, shredded, and burned the fabric of communities. They hadn't wanted me to dispose of Elroy, and they certainly had no intention of doing it. Before I got to him, he'd been in protective custody—*theirs*. But this damned degenerate was a key player in the design of certain drugs; he'd left his safe haven one day, craving a delicacy they'd refused to provide and that he couldn't find nearby. I'd been watching his hidey hole; I knew something was up, but I couldn't see the forest for the tree. I'd ended up cutting the damned tree down, the worst one I could find in the forest, and dragged it out when maybe I should've waited to see if a forest fire had been called for. Shupbach and Watton had gotten wind of my deed, and they knew my MO. They knew that I interrogate people before disposing of them. *Always*. They figured I'd find out something about their operation. Maybe they'd been ready to take me out on the road when they saw me. Or ready to try. Maybe they'd planned to blow up their broken-down car when I got close enough to it for them to knock me out cold. I wouldn't put it past them. They'd been trained as well. The fake couple—the *fakers*. I was their fake love child—the fake soldier—one of many, maybe. Maybe I was just waste to them.

I was now seeing Graham's twisted logic. I didn't like it. I couldn't fully digest it. But it was *in* me.

Raker gave me the run of his place for a few days while he saw to certain arrangements. I spent a few days cleaning, supplying, and decorating a few rooms in the cabin. The man was an avid fisherman, another type of hunter. I'd never learned, but I understood the concept: bait, hooks, lines, and all that. Once I was done with my temporary redecorating, I stood back from it, observing it, mentally working through the uses of its intended abuses. I suspected a casual observer might play the critic and say I'd overdone

it, but I didn't think so. In addition to planning and strategiz-
ing, I also used the time to recuperate and allow myself to
heal as best I could. I tried to push both my mind and body
to razor-sharp condition by maneuvering the course of
hanging dangers, faster and quicker, testing the reflexes. By
the time the day came, my assessment was that both body
and mind had fared well, but of the two it would take much
longer for my mind to fully heal from all this.

Shupbach and Watton arrived a couple of hours ahead
of schedule, driving up in an olive jeep and parking at a
respectable distance. In waders, sun boonies, and fishing
vests, both were well dressed for some fly fishing and
perhaps other sorts of angling. Their arms, necks, and faces
were the only places they exposed their skin. Both carried
wader bags over their shoulders.

I almost shouted to congratulate them on the appropri-
ateness of their gear as I stepped out on the porch, watching
them watch me and their surroundings while pretending
they were only half-interested in either. I was dressed in my
usual casual gear: composite-toe boots, jeans, reinforced
long-sleeve shirt, stocked vest, and specs, which I subtly
adjusted in order to get a *really* good look at them and their
surroundings, ensuring they hadn't invited any others. I saw
nothing, and the sensors Raker had installed on the property weren't raising any alarms, but I was still outnumbered.
Both were very skilled at hand-to-hand combat. They'd have
a fighting chance. *More* than a chance if those wader bags
held what I assumed they did.

"Fishing, huh?" I said as they entered a range where I
could speak and not have my voice carry too far. "Nice
hobby. Catch anything?"

"Not much luck, pal," Schupbach said casually as both
he and Watton continued to nonchalantly cast their eyes

about, searching for signs of anything amiss. "Our cells are out of juice too. We were hoping we could use your landline if you got one."

Who the hell would have a landline out here? I kept the thought to myself and my eyes on them as I nodded. "Out of gas or just lost?"

I opened the door, let them pass, and then closed it behind me.

"You tell us," Schupbach intoned.

"It's secure," I said. "Checked the place over myself."

"Raker's place, huh?" Watton looked about as she shuffled in farther. "*Nice.*"

"Mission accomplished, Sanders?" Schupbach asked.

"Part of it," I said.

"Oh? We understand that Marcus Graham was terminated."

"He was. With extreme prejudice. But he also gave me some information to pass along."

"What information?"

"You first." I guided them toward the living area and, with a gesture, invited them to make themselves comfortable on the couch. They did, placing their bags at their feet, within easy reach. I sat in the arm chair facing them, only appearing to make myself comfortable. "What happened to Elroy?"

"Told you, Frank," Shupbach said. "He's an asset. Nothing we can do."

"So he's free and loose."

Shupbach shook his head. "Under wraps. And inaccessible."

"Sorry, Frank," Watton said.

I got no true sense of regret from her, but I shrugged. "That's okay."

She bent down to open her bag. I watched her closely as she removed some recording equipment. I let my gaze linger as I tried to get a sense of what type of firepower she might be carrying. I raised my eyes when Schupbach cleared his throat. "That information?"

I nodded and then told them everything they needed to know. I condensed the conversations between Graham and me to exchanges of threats and nonsense. Schupbach and Watton seemed to accept it at its face. I certainly kept mine straight during the telling. But I did add one thing at the end. "It's not just Graham. He insisted there are others like him, his family. Higher-end deviants who are getting some high-end outside support—and will *keep* getting support so long as they're useful to those outsiders." I watched their faces closely and listened hard for any changes in their breathing. "Any idea what that might mean?"

Schupbach shrugged and said, "Sounds like more nonsense delivered through some rare complete sentences."

Watton also seemed dismissive as she shut off her equipment and bent to return it to the bag. As she put the equipment away, Schupbach took a deep breath. My eyes flicked between their hands, their vests, and their bags as my muscles tensed, ready for any sudden movements on their behalf.

"Well . . . what are your plans now?" Schupbach seemed to speak with a sense of resignation.

I offered a half smile. "I plan to spend some time up here, in the wilderness, pursuing my favorite hobby." My eyes fell briefly on his bag.

"Fishing?" he said, a little surprised.

"Close." My eyes kept moving; my body remained ready. Their body language wasn't exactly shouting anything—yet. Their eyes were on me, their brows furrowed as if they were genuinely interested in what I had to say and weren't just making small talk. So I said it. "I will be dealing with some slippery creatures. And hooks will be involved."

"Now, Frank, *listen*," Schupbach said, "we've been through this. The government will only afford you so much leeway—"

I held up my hands and gently nodded my head in mock surrender. "Trust me. Those we ultimately answer to will be happy with capture of the evaders of justice I have in mind." So long as I don't have to fillet them first.

Watton cocked her head. "Mind telling us who?"

"Are you talking about Graham's kids?"

I gave them a faint smile. "Maybe. In a twisted sense."

"Frank, stop fucking around."

I glanced at the clock on the coffee table and smiled more fully. "All right. I—" A series of beeps sounded from the kitchen—two short beeps, followed by a longer one. It was Raker, notifying me right on time that he'd successfully contacted one of the knots in his tether to the HSA core, someone much higher up than Schupbach and Watton. Whoever this black agent was, their authority and trustworthiness trumped that of the secret lovers, and the signal meant I had the all-clear to do what I needed to get done.

When I heard the signal, I winced as if it were the whistle to a tea kettle I'd forgotten I'd put on. Once the beeping stopped, Schupbach's heart rate seemed to increase a bit, as if he figured something might be up. Watton seemed oblivious, ignoring the clock on the table to check her own watch.

"Wow," I said. "I've completely forgotten my manners." I stood, heeding the signal's instruction as if it were a parent or teacher trying to smooth out my rude edges. "I forgot to offer you two a drink."

"I'm not thirsty," Schupbach said.

"Well, I am." I glanced toward the kitchen. "I'll need a drink to tell this; and you may need one to hear it."

Schupbach began to ask something, but Watton practically talked over him to ask, "What've you got?"

I favored only one of them with a response as I shook my head and said, "It's not my place, but Raker is a man of discriminating tastes. I'm sure he has something suitable for your palate." I headed toward the kitchen. "Let's see what he's got. You can pick your poison."

Both rose. "We should actually probably get going—" Schupbach began as Watton started after me.

"I could actually use some water."

She'd taken the bait. I grinned. "Figured one of you would." I turned into the kitchen and, ready for the hazards, easily maneuvered to keep myself free of them as I mumbled, "Just like a fish."

"Huh?" Watton said as she began to turn the corner. "What do you—"

She stopped cold; her eyes almost seemed to glaze over as they took in the contraptions I'd set up.

Mere steps away from her but separated by several hanging hooks and barbed fishing lines, I muttered, "You two, I know, are very familiar with strings and hooks..."

Her hand was in her vest before I could even punctuate the sentence; I wasted no time being proper, using it instead to close the distance, duck in, and strike the heel of my palm under her chin. A mere punch to the head, she would've expected—or at least reflexively rolled with while grabbing her gun. This was a blow she wasn't expecting; it had the added bonus of slamming her teeth together, keeping her on her feet but stunning her just long enough for me to snatch her hand out of her vest—sans gun—and swing her into the kitchen. I maneuvered in quickly, dancing with her, taking possession of her firearm, tying her up, tangling her in barbed wires, and plunging hooks deep into her exposed flesh and deeper into her clothing.

She shrieked through it all, and through all her cries I heard the commotion in the other room—Schupbach opening his tackle box, retrieving his weapon of choice, and cautiously rushing in our direction. My hand was on Watton's semiautomatic and my body was behind hers before her boyfriend appeared in the entranceway. I put a bullet in his right knee before he could even begin to assess the situation. I disarmed him with another shot to the elbow before he had a clue. By the time I was on him, he seemed to have an inkling.

He was a big guy, but I could handle him—though he proved to be less of a dancer, more of a bleeder. I had to pistol whip him a little to get him compliant enough to move as I wanted. But in no time at all, relatively speaking, I had both of them caught up—just as, Graham claimed, they'd metaphorically intended for me.

Their anguished grunts and cries of pain didn't stop, what with the hooks deep in their flesh—painful at rest, even more so when those who were caught up struggled to get themselves free. But amid the noise, they each managed to shout out complete sentences, short questions, and longer threats, mostly along the lines of whether I was crazy and if I understood what was going to happen to me because of this. Schupbach even had the audacity to mention that I was still, indirectly, a government agent, and this was somehow treasonous.

I sidled up to him. "Let me make something perfectly clear to you. I have no allegiance to any nation. No country, no formal religion, no ethnicity, no *bullshit*."

"You have an oath!" Watton shouted, her hoarse voice making her sound far more feral than human.

"And you," I said, "are the reason humankind has not reached its potential. You are Satan's keeper; you are breeders of Satan's spawn. You have consulted or consorted with the other realm to bring about this plague of rapacious, murderous deviants. You've traded. I'm sure you've paid a fee. But there's also a tax."

"You're crazy!" Schupbach shouted for the sixth or seventh time. "We haven't done *anything!*"

"We'll see. I'm a fair man. I know you well enough to know you have methods of concealing the truth. But I have methods of revealing hidden truths."

"*Frank!*" Watton began.

"Oh, and about that oath . . . There's a little misunderstanding about that." I circled them, maneuvered between the wires. "The oath is made up of words, but without action, it's lifeless. I have chosen my side. This little exercise will be to see whose side you're really on. If I'm wrong, if I go beyond the bounds, I have no issue with offering myself up as a sacrifice."

"You *dumb* son of a *bitch*—you're *dead!*"

"I will *personally* do your injections!"

"You will . . . what?" Something red-violet flashed behind my eyes. Already we were getting somewhere, but I had to hold myself in check and do this right. I chuckled as I continued circling. "Tell me, *lovers*, have either of you ever seen two anglerfish mating?"

"*What?*"

"You're *insane!*"

"Lips fused, one's skin becoming the other's, organs dissolving, one's blood becoming the other's . . ."

"*Goddamn it, Sanders!*"

"Just my way of saying all secrets are now over." I stopped circling and stood so they could both get a good look at me and me at them. "All right, flirty fishies—let's get started."

I was about two miles away from Cordero's, cooling my tires at a red light. It was just after lunchtime. I was hoping Frankie was already full—and not with too much junk food. I was hoping even more that she hadn't forgotten who I was. And even if she had, I hoped she'd be enticed back home with the new, handmade doll that was now warming The Machine's front passenger seat.

I had actually found it in Krissy's vehicle with a note. She'd intended to give it to me after the hunt was over. Frankly, it wasn't over—and she and Juliano would never be forgotten. But I'd have to try to push the memory of them to the back of my mind when I faced my little girl. She deserved no worries. Only smiles, grins, laughs, and hugs— lots of warm hugs.

I didn't get all the answers I wanted from Schupbach and Watton, but I got enough to settle on a few other characters to examine. My oath wouldn't need any addenda— but I would need to add a new prong between my sanctioned hunts and my hobby. Maybe I'd call it a "submission" or an inquisition. Maybe.

The light turned green just as my smartphone buzzed. I glanced at it and saw a number that intrigued me, enough so that I pulled into the nearest fast-food parking lot in order to give it my full attention.

My oath was printed across the wallpaper of my smartphone. I skimmed it from time to time, but presently I took the opportunity to read it in full, with full presence of mind, in the space between receiving the notification and reading the text from Trent Harwood. His message told me which body parts he wanted sent to him—or, more precisely, to his wife.

Elroy was temporarily out of my custody; in the meantime, I hoped Ethel and my one-time boss would be satisfied with a few replacements. I figured *he* would be, at least. A chief that had to deal with a city as bad as Garth would know all about chains of command—big fish, little fish, and all that.

ABOUT THE SERIES

When their bodies are overwhelmed by an onslaught of parasites that feed on blood and light, most victims of the White Fire Virus die quickly but in excruciating pain. They could be considered the lucky ones. Those who survive continue to live on in physical and psychological torment; they also find themselves endowed with a range of supernatural abilities. Many of these survivors consider themselves angels, potential saviors of humanity. Others want nothing less than the death of God. And there are a few who are even more ambitious.

Eve of Light is a dark metaphysical fantasy—philosophical, intense, action-packed, and *surreal*.

The Core Novels

BloodLight: The Apocalypse of Robert Goldner
Broken Angels (Eve of Light Book I)
Divinities, Entangled (Eve of Light Book II)

The Deviant-Hunter Stories

Deviant-Hunter: Blood Oath
Deviant-Hunter, Killer of Saints
Deviant-Hunter's Sabbath

Other Stories on the Fringe

FoolKillers
The Lark
Heaven's Gun
Knotty & Ice
Rogue Beauty

ABOUT THE AUTHOR

Harambee K. Grey-Sun writes under the broad umbrella of speculative fiction. He integrates elements of fantasy, horror, noir, black humor, and science fiction into his work, spinning tales that are dark, surreal, mysterious, grotesque, at times challenging, and—some would even say—blasphemous. His dark metaphysical fantasy series, Eve of Light, examines the dark nature of God and what it really means to be human.

For more information:

Click Here for Author's Website
www.harambeegreysun.com

ALSO BY HARAMBEE K. GREY-SUN

Standalone Stories

Beholder

Love Among the Ultramoderns

Unfair Play

Last Contact

The Lure

The *EVE OF LIGHT* Series

The Novels

BloodLight: The Apocalypse of Robert Goldner (*Prequel*)

Broken Angels (*Book I*)

Divinities, Entangled (*Book II*)

The Novellas

Deviant-Hunter: Blood Oath

Deviant-Hunter, Killer of Saints

Deviant-Hunter's Sabbath

The Short Stories

Hell's Brood (*A Collection*)

BY HARAMBEE GREY-SUN

Poetry

Spring's Fall (Autumn Numbers * Book I)

Wine Songs, Vinegar Verses